Pa

Acknowledgements

My appreciation to my wife Gayle, who continued to encourage me to keep writing.

My thanks to Matthew Clark and Douglas Moses who were my proof readers and technical consultants. Any errors are mine that I failed to correct.

Paradise Above

A science fiction story of danger and intrigue. Eight members of SSI, Inc. aboard the Space Station PARADISE, must make desperate decisions regarding their survival. Earth-side, a DNA altering plague sweeps across the globe, their only true lifeboat. Survival will depend on trust and cooperation, a rare commodity aboard the space station as two individuals will insist they are the rightful COS, or Commander of Station.

Several of the scientists were to be replaced as SSI's shuttle Endeavor-3 arrives with new personnel, but the plague places all of them on the same team despite their fears and hostilities. Each member of the team has known and unknown reasons for placing their loyalty elsewhere. Who will anyone trust? Information from Earth becomes scarcer each day as contacts begin to fail.

The usually reliable computer systems begin to act strangely regarding who can access information. The station's computer specialist claims to be working on it, but most believe he is the cause of the changes and issues.

The station personnel must make several critical decisions regarding their survival. How long can they stay in space? When and how should they return to Earth? What kind of alliance of co-operation can they form with the Russian and Japanese space stations?

Who can be trusted to guide them to safety?

Cast of Significant Characters:

Crew
**Shuttle
Endeavor 3**   Matthew Rogers, senior pilot 6 years, age 30
Janice Wells, co-pilot 1st year, age 28

Passengers
**Shuttle
Endeavor 3**   Steven Holt, new COS, replacing Pavel, age 31
Miki Yew, R&D/Biology/Medical, replacing Sid, age 24

Crew
PARADISE   Pavel Oberholtz, current COS, Russian, age 55
Sid Voorhies, R&D/Environmental, age 36
Blade Stormecky, Computer/Data Systems, age 27
Laura Houle, Science/Medical, age 30

Crew
**MIRROR
Station**   Annushka Rusnak, Commander of Station, age 36
Stepan Barkov, 2nd in command, age 38

SSI
Earth   Ben Johnson, Flight Operations, SSI, Inc, age 32
James Donaldson, Director, North America age 49

Paradise Above

Table of Contents

Prologue

It's mid-21st century and all reasons for establishing space stations for military or space exploration have diminished largely due to economics. However, a handful of industrial companies have developed smaller versions for their own research and manufacturing processes. One company, Space Sciences Inc. (SSI), has developed a space station named **PARADISE** which they use for their company research. SSI allows other companies to share it for fees. SSI developed it's own shuttle technology and has three orbital vehicles, all capable of runway take-off and landing. Rockets are no longer utilized for Earth orbit trajectories or missions. Multiple countries and companies have such shuttle technology since most zero gravity space research is done from these vehicles.

There are two other similar "pseudo-private" space stations in orbit.

The Russian one, **MIRROR**, is assumed to be a cover for the government's own research and initiatives. While space based weapons have been banned for years and satellite observations have been perfected by better methods than a space station, what the Russians are developing is most analysts' guess, but of no general world interest except to several secret government agencies. **MIRROR** has five shuttles, three for transport to its station and two strictly for zero gravity research. Several shuttles have been grounded for more than six months, far longer than normal maintenance schedules.

The third space station in orbit is the Japanese, publicly owned, **SUNSTAR**. Several Pan-Asian companies cleverly control the finances and actual operations. While the secret technology of this research station is enough to confound the sharpest of minds, few can doubt the success in new products and patents they have reaped over the last several years. **SUNSTAR** has just one functioning shuttle and one in assembly dock. No timeframe to be in service has been released to the public or investors.

The Stage

SSI has just sent the shuttle Endeavor-3, with veteran pilot Matthew Rogers and rookie pilot Janice Wells, who are bringing two replacement crewmembers to the space station. Steve Holt is to replace Pavel Oberholtz as the new Commander of Station, in charge of all operations on the space platform. Miki Yew, an American of Japanese descent, is the new Medical and Biological Researcher. The company was to replace Laura Houle; however, SSI decision makers had decided at the last minute to replace Sid Voorhies who has been falling out of favor with top company officials over policy and procedures. Sid is not going to be happy with this and will be resentful and less supportive of anything having to do with SSI. There are unproven rumors that someone is selling SSI's industrial secrets to other competing companies.

In route to PARADISE, a biological "event" occurs on Earth, where a DNA altering plague is spreading rapidly that causes the brain to shut down, resulting in a loss of biological functions and a quick death. This plaque will sweep across the Earth in about three weeks. There is little detail on this as it spreads so fast and is so deadly, that no one can provide any accurate information on it, except to speculate. This will only add to the confusion and desperation in which the characters will have to plan their next moves.

This leads to a real conflict as to who is in fact the Commander of Station(COS), since Pavel will want to continue leadership through experience and seniority. Steve Holt is the new generation of space worker, who is a clear thinker, risk taker, better at getting people to work together, and less authoritarian. He has documents that show he is the new COS, and of course Pavel was to return to Earth, which is temporarily impossible.

Matt Rogers - Will take a back seat to no one while in space and is commander of the shuttle that will be a key element in their survival. He doesn't like or trust Pavel, but he has little working experience with the new COS Holt.

Blade Stormecky - Or 'Storm" for a nickname, is the computer genius. While most "spacers" have considerable computer skills and are comfortable with computer systems, none can match or try to duplicate what "Storm" can do so easily. He had designed portions of the computer systems used onboard PARADISE. In addition, he is constantly tinkering with software systems to improve them, even loading and changing versions without permission from ground control. This will not set well with Ben Johnson when or if he finds out.

Ben Johnson - A personal friend to Matt, is in charge of shuttle operations and safety. He provides insights into the disaster and will be one of the few contacts from Earth that the station can trust. He will assist the station-bound crew on information regarding the spread of the plague and will lead the effort to return the crew to Earth when possible.

Endeavor-3 - SSI's shuttle Endeavor-3 consists of four 'bays' or sections. The upper compartment doors do not open as in previous shuttle versions. There is no extending arm to maneuver to place or retrieve objects in space. SSI custom built their shuttles specifically for their own industrial needs.

Pilot's Bay – Or command section is where the flight instrumentation and pilots are located.

Passenger/Experimental Bay – This is the 'main cabin'; passenger seats are mounted for exactly the number of passengers at launch. The rest of this section is utilized for zero-gravity experiments. Work tables are assembled and pre-mounted for scheduled work. SSI does a few experiments here, but most are conducted on PARADISE. This is the area that is leased out to other companies that do not have Earth orbit shuttles. Charges are not by the hour, but by the number of rotations of the Earth flown. Passengers and/or staff can sleep comfortably here if pre-configured for extended stay. Docking is thru the docking ring located on the starboard side of this section. This requires Endeavor to dock alongside PARADISE or other stations.

Cargo Bay – Or 'payload' section. Supplies, hardware, or instruments are secured in this section for transport to Earth or station side.

Engine Bay – There is no easy access to this area. Secondary fuel tanks are in the wings, but feed into a central fuel tank located below the main cabin.

SSI's Endeavor-3

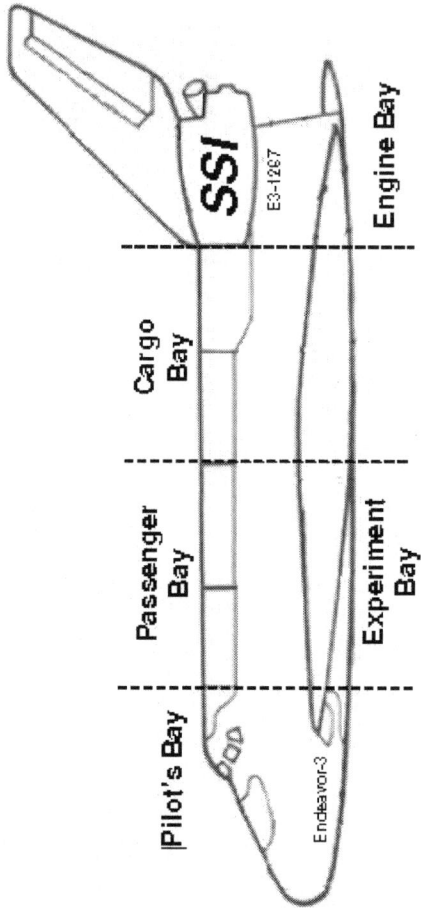

Engine Bay

Cargo Bay

Passenger Bay

Experiment Bay

Pilot's Bay

SSI

E3-1267

Endeavor-3

Endeavor-3 shown port side

SSI's PARADISE Station

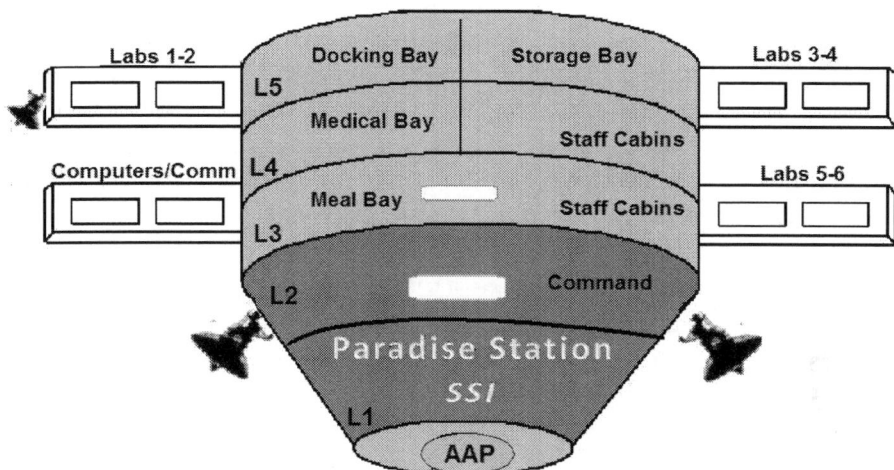

Labs 1-2 — Docking Bay | Storage Bay — **Labs 3-4**
L5
Medical Bay | Staff Cabins
Computers/Comm L4 — **Labs 5-6**
Meal Bay | Staff Cabins
L3
L2 | Command
Paradise Station
SSI
L1
AAP

SSI PARADISE station, serial # - OS0045

Set in orbit, June 20th, 2042, PARADISE was initially fifty-nine tons of frame and structure, and nine tons of laboratory equipment, computers and life support systems. The station was upgraded in 2048 with increased laboratory space, artificial gravity inducers, two new labs and additional living areas.

Chapter 1   Big Blue Marble

Endeavor-3 – Pilot Bay   09:15 am Nov 4

It does look like a big blue marble, thought Janice Wells, as she gazed out the co-pilot's window while the Earth was rotating towards her vehicle. The silver and blue shuttle had just reached minimal Earth orbit level and the two pilots began the first revolution flight procedures. She estimated she had little more than a minute and a half before her flight screens required her to be mentally heads-down into the next set of flight maneuvers. While Matt, the command pilot of their shuttle Endeavor-3, had the most critical tasks to perform, her procedures were no less vital to a safe orbit and docking maneuver with SSI's station, PARADISE. Senior pilots often spoke of their similar experience on their maiden flight. She would have just this short time where she could observe the world as only God probably did. She fully intended to drink it all in.

She'd seen the same view a dozen times from various satellites, but in her heart, she hoped it would be different somehow. This was her turn to observe with her own eyes the world that seemed so immense when you tried to traverse it by anything other than Earth orbit. She vaguely remembered her frustrations as a child when she had to move from country to country with her parents. The distances seemed beyond her young mind to comprehend. That did not last long. Janice had a determined spark that resented anything she couldn't totally comprehend. It was the secret drive that propelled her through all the sciences and studies that instructors could throw at her. She mastered them all with an ease that baffled most educators at every level. But space was her last mystery. Janice held a deep and hidden conviction that no one would be her teacher about space. She would be her own master. That determined conviction brought her to Flight School within Space Sciences Inc. But this was the moment every pilot told her would happen. No matter how big your dreams or aspirations, this was when you really saw your place in the universe. Often it humbled you and sometimes it inspired you past the dreams and aspirations of your youth. It was the moment for every flight officer on their first trip into the hostile barrier encircling the home world. How it would affect Janice was still undetermined, even in her own mind. She just sat there unspeaking, unmoving with the same glassy-eyed stare that mimicked every pilot before her, unaware that she had been holding her breath.

Matt watched his rookie co-pilot with a grin in his thoughts if not on his face. He bet Ben fifty bucks Janice would not go into the "first flight catatonic" stage he observed from his peripheral vision. He was so sure she would perform with the efficient clockwork precision she tackled every previous assignment. The bet was supposed to be a sure thing.

"Control, this is E-3, completed MEO and beginning second rev."

"Roger E3, Minimal Earth Orbit complete," sounded mechanically thru Matt's comm-link within a few seconds.

"Tell BJ, he won, E3 out," Matt continued. He released the comm membrane switch again, which toggled back to receive.

"Roger that E3, we show green and go on all mission boards, all flight procedures. Commlink if you need something. Your glide path is ninety–eight percent to track, course adjustment on next go-round. Control out." There was a calm silence as Matt reviewed a fuel gage, engine temp, and several tracking instruments that indicated the status of the vehicle.

"It was a sure thing," cracked a tired voice into his helmet speaker. "How long?"

I knew this call was coming, Matt thought.

"She's still in it, maybe sixty seconds," said Matt. This time he did smile. It didn't matter what the amount was, losing a bet to Ben Johnson was ok. They had joined SSI about the same time, even though their career goals were at opposite altitudes. Their friendship started close and grew as close as brothers, which neither had. While Matt's drive was focused solely on traversing Earth orbits, Ben's were on operations and safety. He ran the flight OPS, mission planning, and absolutely anything that had to do with shuttle safety.

While Ben never spoke about it, Matt suspected Ben's personal drive related to losing his father in a space shuttle accident twenty-five years ago. The investigation had pointed no fingers publicly, but Ben had held suspicions in several internal areas. Despite that loss, having Ben Johnson managing your flight was akin to "swinging in your mama's arms". You knew the issues were covered, and backups to backups were in place and tested. You didn't want to be on the wrong side of BJ on a safety report. Once and you were reprimanded. Twice and you were no longer in the department.

"Your fifty bucks are in an envelope with your name on it. Look in the top shelf of my locker. See you Thursday and you can buy me a steak dinner at RIBS," said Matt; just now realizing that his leaving the money in advance could be interpreted as not having the confidence in Janice he really felt. But Ben wouldn't think of that.

"Oh no you don't. You've got to put the bills in my hand, so you can see the big smile on my face as you count them out." Ben replied back. "Enough chit chat, you've got several tests and an altitude correction coming up. Back to work, fly boy, Johnson out."

"What was that?" Janice mumbled, her space funk starting to dissolve as she attempted to sit up straighter, constraining against the shoulder straps that already had her in the proper position for flight but were cutting into her shoulders slightly.

"Just Ben.....reviewing some procedures," Matt said, trying to keep a straight face and hoping his helmet would conceal visibly what he couldn't in his voice.

"Did you win the bet?" Janice asked, as if inquiring about something as simple as the weather.

"What bet?" Matt replied, trying to deflect his embarrassment by tapping two panel switches that made no real difference.

"I don't know, but Kevin said you and Johnson bet something on every one of your flights, but he doesn't bet on anything else. Or with anyone else, just you." Janice maintained a calm, but inquiring tone, as she checked off her next set of procedures as co-pilot.

"Well, I lost," Matt whispered, trying to deflate the conversation, by lack of power in his voice.

"Bet on a sure thing, did you?" Janice whispered back, with the cutest smile Matt had ever seen as she turned her head to face him. "There's no such thing," she continued, with just a trace of humor embedded.

"So far, I agree with you, but that won't stop me from searching for it," Matt said so quietly only he could hear it. His light blue eyes rested on the sexiest person he'd ever met. After twelfth grade that is, as he reminisced, with his own smile breaking out again. His helmet speaker broke his momentary daydream.

"Going to procedure R, as in Roger, two," he heard Janice thru his helmet. Matt cleared his thoughts and replied,

"Check. R2. Complete those procedures and let Steve and Miki know we dock with PARADISE in about fifty minutes. By the book, you should contact PARADISE, although Blade will have been tracking us since we left the break room this morning. I'm beginning the orbital tests and a minor course adjustment on control's mark."

Matt was relieved to retreat back into the routine of flight altitudes, fuel consumption and vector angles. Shuttle subjects in his domain where he was confident. Not so with romantic words or gestures that seemed foreign to the thirty-year-old bachelor. Matt had sporadic dates, and a few love interests that could have developed farther but never did. Matt couldn't remember why or deemed to care. They were never the right one he kept telling himself.

But Janice appeared to be the kind of woman he thought he was looking for. He had been observing her, cautiously, throughout her eighteen-month training. Matt mentally checked off her attributes that appealed to him and a dozen other co-workers by the conversations he overheard. *Intelligence wrapped in common sense, strong willed, but with the openness to listen to other opinions. Focused and determined about projects and her work, but at ease with any social group inside or out of the company. All that and well packaged besides.*

Matt never went for glamour and beauty queen stuff. Beauty for him was simple and efficient, like a good shuttle design. Janice, at five-seven, a hundred ten pounds, brownish red hair, cut so short that it focused you to her impish face, was a superior design. Brown eyes that sparkled and a smile that always conveyed one trait. Mischievous. She didn't mind being the center of attention, but didn't seek it, being confident in who she was and what she was doing. Matt had quickly determined that she was indeed what he was looking for, but patiently waited and watched her from afar. Their assignment together was no accident, although their eventual teaming would certainly have happened within a few more months. Matt carefully applied the right comments here and there to make it happen sooner. He was ready for the next step and wanted the opportunity to work with her in a closer manner.

I'll be trying to file that flight path soon. Not today or tomorrow, but soon, he thought. *I may still be searching for my sure thing, but I'm definitely locked on target.*

"Control, this is E3. We are ready for course adjustment, starboard engine, three second burn, on your mark," Matt relayed into his mic. He was mentally back, full throttle to the mission, the one place SSI expected their top pilot to be. He had a childhood habit of not disappointing those who depended on him.

Chapter 2   Storm Center

Blade Stormecky's eyes were riveted to his computer console screen absorbing every digit and graphical change as if his brain were plugged directly into the monitor and bypassing his visual senses. He noticed that E3's tracking path was ninety-seven point seven percent of target, rather than the ninety-eight he heard the ground control officer relay to the shuttle pilot.

"Humans," he murmured. "So imprecise when the actual numbers are right there on their screens in front of their faces." He knew the pilot, Rogers, would adjust perfectly and thought he was the closest thing to a human processor he'd encountered. Including most of the college computer nerds he'd hung with in earlier days. Cool and precise. An opinion he shared with no one.

Of course he rarely shared opinions on anything with anyone. Data was different. Data was pure. He'd share data. Data should belong to everyone. His feelings and thoughts belonged to him alone, and no level of password access could make him reveal what thoughts were stored behind his thick brown hair and eyes so dark brown they appeared black in low light. This was just the way he liked it in his private quarters. The only light source in his nine meter by nine meter living space was the cold greenish glow emanating from his console, and even that was turned down low. Most of the crew was loath to come into his "sanctuary", which was just fine. Blade keyed a few additional commands into the console, waited and reviewed the results that he anticipated and logged off.

"It was a pleasure serving you," offered a sexy voice from his console speakers. He grinned as he thought about the recent changes he had made in the system's operating system interface, and wondered who would be the first to know and who would be the first to complain. He switched off the screen and headed to the OPS center of the station to inform his "Pavelness" that Endeavor would be docking on schedule. Everyone on PARADISE knew what that meant. He was hoping to see the look on Pavel's face when it finally sunk in that his COS duty was over. He was sure that would cause a few of Pavel's teeth to grind, and he sure wanted to be the one to set that in motion.

Pavel, it's time to re-boot you and start a new program, thought Blade. It was the most pleasing thought he could remember since he intercepted the audio and video session when Pavel received his walking papers. *Yes, it was a very good thought*, he pondered, as he closed his eyes and having no desire to change the gleaming smile that was working across his unshaven face.

With you gone, I can focus on my other target, because I don't believe for a minute that Sid is leaving. Not the way Sid is talking or acting.

PARADISE Station – Command Center   09:21 am Nov 4

Pavel Oberholtz was lost in thought as he sat in the commander's chair, the center of attention in the station's op center. His dark features, dark beard and hair belied his fifty-five years. Many his age had begun the "greying effect", but Pavel's hair was the same shade when he was twenty. A quirk of genetics? His more youthful appearance allowed him little trouble in commanding attention or this station. That was however, before the announcement from HQ. Pavel was the third "Commander of Station" for SSI's space research platform, PARADISE. He had held the title nearly twice as long as either of his predecessors combined. Pavel was COS almost three years with the last two years of continuous service since the gravity generators were added and crew no longer had to return to Earth for two months out of the year. The efficiency gained with the gravity, was remarkable, but Pavel was sure it wasn't his lack of performance or the station's that were the real reasons for his removal. A new wave of investors and managers of SSI had a different path in mind for their operations and a new breed of staff was being chosen to follow it. Pavel apparently was not in their future space-based plans. *What would he do next?* He'd been thinking about that almost all of his waking hours since he received the news last week. He was aware a maintenance shuttle had been scheduled to bring supplies and some new processors for Stormecky's system upgrades. They usually don't make a flight until the payload warrants it. There were some experiment results to return to base, but again, not enough to merit a launch. His manager, Donaldson, had surprised him with details of new procedures for manufacturing of the key pharmaceuticals they were developing.

Then he slipped in the news of replacing Sid for performance reasons. Pavel had laughed as he readily agreed to the reasoning and timing. Yes, Miki Yew will be a wonderful replacement he thought. Neither man spoke for an unusually long pause.

"Was-------there anything else?" Pavel remembered asking the loaded question with a slight fear. He was getting proficient at reading the man's voice. His manager cleared his throat and dropped the bombshell, which just likely exploded his space career to nothingness.

"Ah, Pavel, we will be asking you to step down as well. I can't elaborate the exact reasons right now, but I assure you---- we will discuss them at great length. There are some suspicions and a few accusations floating around, but I am told they have not been verified. I know this comes as a shock, without warning. The directors wanted me to pass on their thanks for all the work you have done, and to assure you of a position with SSI here in Texas once all these issues get ironed out. Your replacement is Steve Holt who I think you already know from your time together in Berlin. Please begin preparing the transition reports for Steve. I look forward to seeing you next week. I will contact Sid and review these changes with him myself," he added. While only fifteen seconds passed, it seemed like an eternity.

"Pavel, don't take this too hard. I need a man like you right here with me and you'll have your choice of several positions. Let's get these rumors behind us and we can concentrate on what's next for you. Whatever you want to try, we'll get it done. We'll speak again before that. Donaldson out."

Pavel had to admit, it was the smoothest firing he'd ever experienced. The knot in his stomach that had started the moment he switched off his view screen that day, still had not diminished. The crew seemed to know within the hour, and now four days later, both he and Sid were treated with little more than a civil nod or murmur when discussing operational procedures. As if his opinion no longer carried any weight, which is precisely the way it is, he surmised.

He had immediately considered his employment options and the Russian space station MIRROR came to mind. He recalled some contacts and favors he might pursue. Slowly, but surely, the Russian opportunity dissolved as he mentally weighed all the factors. Of course the Japanese SUNSTAR was not even remotely possible, so that left a career change or hanging around Houston until retirement. Neither option appeared to raise his hope. Pavel began to feel like an old relic while simultaneously being at the top of his field. A high tech situation occurring more often these days he imagined.

And what was Donaldson hinting at? What suspicions? What accusations? At that moment the smirking face of Stormecky interrupted his thoughts.

"What do you want?" growled Pavel in a low volume tone and manner. Blade hadn't perceived his lips even moved though he had been looking right into Pavel's face. This was an example of the cold and impersonal manner Pavel used when he did not want to be bothered or even involved in a conversation that was being forced upon him.

"I just wanted to inform you that Endeavor should be docking with us at about nine hundred thirty hours, right on schedule. I thought you'd like to know," Blade said, trying to keep his internal ear-to-ear grin from registering on his lean and oblong face.

"So now I know," replied Pavel, with no change in his facial expression or the slightest movement in his chair. "You may return to your work and be sure to complete the computer system's report by twelve hundred hours that I asked for yesterday." Pavel continued to look at the overhead computer monitor. Several moments passed as each man appeared frozen and unmovable. Pavel finally swiveled again to face his subordinate and looked him square in the eyes.

"Mr. Stormecky?" This time there was no attempt at disguising the contempt he felt for the computer technician and

PARADISE came as a shock, would require a revision to the word.

Sid brushed his fingers over the top of his head, a certain sign of his frustration that even he was unaware. His hair was cut between a butch on top and shaved bald-like on the sides, leaving a Mohawk effect, which was strange looking, but ideal for space. In limited lighting, the faintly golden and smallish portion of his hair made him seem completely bald. The sinister effect was heightened by the small gray eyes deeply buried into a smaller than average head, resting on the shortest man in space science. Sid indeed had influence and power but it was packed into the smallest human frame in the industry. He was aware of the meeting jokes and sideline remarks, but they lost their power when he didn't react. Power has many forms and the First Rule of Sid was, "it's not really power until it can be applied at the right time and place". Sid was sure he could have turned this situation around if he had more time. It was the very first time he had been caught unaware and subject to changes he had not controlled. He hummed some meaningless tune while he sealed the two containers, wondering why he had bothered. He did not intend for them to be placed aboard the Endeavor.

Not on this flight. No, I have other plans. And plans within plans, wandered thru his thoughts.

Yes, change was hurtling toward him, which was undeniable. But change that he controlled was not something to fear, but rather to be enjoyed. He just had to get control of this. He pushed the containers beneath his bunk with his foot and turned toward his computer screen. He pressed the green logon button and was taken aback by the sexy voice admonition to "please login". He smiled cautiously. His console screen already contained his user name, so he only had to retype his password. He entered the eight-character security code and was greeted with a flashing invalid logon and a verbal "user name is no longer valid," which was no longer sexy or friendly.

"Stormecky," he shouted in rage as he slammed his fist down on the keyboard. ***Control-------control, I must remain calm and in control***, he thought, clenching his teeth and imagining himself choking Stormecky. He took several deep breaths and tried to relax his body, starting with his shoulders. He pressed a wall panel switch that activated a voice channel to the command center.

"Commander Pavel, can I have a word with you?" Audibly they were calm words, but their sound smashed frustration and desperation together. They sounded like poison to the well informed.

"I'm in the control room, I can meet with you in ten minutes," crackled back thru the panel. With that, Sid trudged off to the control room, careful to bypass Stormecky's cabin. There was a heavy lift to his gait as he moved with a measured step. Deliberate, cautious and vengeful.

Cross me once and you'll pay. Cross me again and you'll be sorry you did it the first time, Sid's vindictive reflections smashed through his consciousness replacing his usual planning thoughts. It was his one fault. When angry, his thinking leaned to revenge, and his normally careful and precise planning had very rough edges. Edges where people tended to get hurt.

Chapter 4　　Commanders & Compromises

　　　　Steven Thomas Holt appreciated the efficiency of the new shuttle technology that enabled liftoff to station docking in slightly less than four hours, but secretly preferred the previous flight paths that provided a bit more time to be a tourist in space. The newer shuttles and trajectories, the latest of everything that SSI threw into their core business was all geared to save time, money and show investors an increasingly strong financial bottom line. Steve was all for that as a significant portion of his compensation package was tied into stock options and company performance. But newer wasn't always better when considering all viewpoints. That is exactly what Steve wanted to do more of; see the Earth from every viewpoint possible, because until two years ago, standard orbital flights used to take more than six hours and multiple rotations.

　　　　He frequently had the opportunity to observe the Black Forest where his grandparents lived and recalled fond memories of playing "Robin Hood" in his youth. He was usually the leader, not because he was bigger or stronger than anyone else. It was solely his ability to compromise and suggest a new way to get all the boys involved in the games. This skill was so natural Steve was hardly aware of exercising it and rarely did it offend his peers. He just liked getting everyone to work or play together, and by observing people's verbal and physical reactions to options, he was usually able to explain the plans or games that combined elements that all could accept. He developed and refined this skill in virtually all aspects of his personal and work groups and used it to further a successful career in space technologies, where compromising was the active watch word. He was blessed with many complementing skills that formed the basis for his interaction with both personal and business contacts. There was no question he had an above average IQ, which was necessary for most space-based positions. Steve's strength was a solid open mind with intuitive technical experience that invoked the right questions in the right manner. He displayed a calm and reassuring manner that was easy to follow no matter how critical the current situation might appear. People inherently believed and acted on the theory that, 'follow Steve' was the best action to take for those concerned. This was certainly the high point of his career, COS of the most admired industrial space station. *But what about after that? There didn't seem to be anything greater than this opportunity and what would he do next? Man, this gig might last several years, but I gotta be planning my next move now.* His mind was whirling with conflicting thoughts.

Miki Yew was restless. Restless in her restraints, her spirit and her thinking. She felt as locked up in her life as these shoulder restraints had her locked into her shuttle seat. The last forty-eight hours were "blur-city". She had dozens of scheduled medical tests and research papers that would have thoroughly squeezed all of her time for the next six months. Then the 'Word' came down. *Crashing down was more accurate*, she thought,

Miki was supposed to replace Renata, who was supposed to replace Laura Houle on the space station. But some last minute, high-level, uber-decision, had changed all the medical planning and direction for the company. She was now heading to PARADISE to take over the medical testing/R&D support from Voorhies. This was a high profile position, not something she was seeking for at least several more years. Why did they pick her? In fact, she would have been perfectly happy to be Earth-bound and just beneath headquarters' radar for another year. Miki had turned over all her files, documents and strategy charts to her partner, Sam, and wished him luck. He'll be sleepless for the next several weeks trying to co-ordinate all the projects they both had going until he gets some support.

Why this change? Why replace Voorhies? She wondered. He was considered to be the top-notch R&D researcher in the industry; especially to hear him expound on his achievements. Others spoke volumes of his inflated ego, but no one questioned his skills. Miki had worked with him two years ago on a joint project. He was knowledgeable and efficient, even if somewhat cold. He seemed to focus only on the project and nothing else. That seemed to mold perfectly into the new company manager's strategy. Everyone said he was the rising star if he didn't ruin his own path. Miki closed her datapad without making any further notes to all the files on Voorhies' projects. Her first twenty-four hours would be pretty straight forward. Get acclimated to the station, understand how the new COS works and prioritize the projects that Voorhies had initiated. All the while, playing it cool. This new position was not what she had planned for. She had just begun planning her wedding and all the myriad details of dresses, cakes, flowers and family. The last was going to be the trickiest of all knowing her father. She barely got to say goodbye to Kwan, and not even in person. He was unreachable until almost two hours after launch. Their "private video" was unlikely private and she knew enough not to speak openly about their engagement. Miki could not even tell Kwan how long this assignment would be, since she received no reasonable answer to that question herself for the past two days.

Ok, a short term compromise. But she better have an answer soon as to how long she had to be in space on this assignment. They want medical reactions in space? She'll give them all they could handle if she wasn't walking down an aisle in white satin within the next six months!

Chapter 5   Mysterious News

PARADISE station appeared to Janice like a huge white child's tinker toy. Its detail was in stark contrast to the blackness of space that surrounded it from most angles. Even though it appeared so massive, she knew it was only the third largest of the current stations in orbit. PARADISE was even smaller than the two platform stations currently under construction, and scheduled to launch within the next two years. Another corporate station and another country station, both from the European Sector. But stations are not gauged by the size of the platform alone. The station staff, the transport shuttles, the base staff, the scientists and funding all have an effect on what's significant. PARADISE incorporated all that and carried with their banner of success a bit of industrial envy.

Since she had not been on PARADISE station prior, she had briefly studied the initial build and the several modifications of seventy three tons of frame and another twelve tons of industrial equipment it housed. She found it difficult to think of PARADISE just as a set of labs. The marketing brochures portrayed it more like a cozy home away from home and she bought in to some of it. In a few minutes she would walk it's corridors and breathe it's chambered air. While that thought set her heart stirring just a little bit, she mentally flushed all those images so she could concentrate on their approach to the Earth-side docking ring. Matt was using minimal thrusters as he nudged the craft horizontally to the magnetic locking ring on the side of PARADISE. She heard the quiet "metallic clunk" as clamps secured about the same time she saw the docking indicators illuminate.

"Docked and locked," Janice uttered quietly, hoping she remembered correctly one of the dozens of phrases the pilots and instructors had gone over with her at SSI training. Simple and clear were the stressed commands for pilot communication where one mistaken phrase had more than once caused some serious issues.

"Docked systems engaged, flight systems off," she addressed her captain with precise and minimal words. She depressed two switches and confirmed the status lights indicating the docking state. All that was left was to check the door seals and pressure sensors which she would do manually as a backup safety procedure, despite the main console showing all "green". SSI was a stickler for procedures; and procedures were golden rule number one.

Matt turned to Janice and gave her a short, but polite command, "Why don't you assist in getting our passengers unstrapped and their gear ready to unload. Blade will likely, as usual; have a cart positioned right outside the docking door for his systems hardware and PARADISE's main supplies. I'll finish up the minor shutdown procedures and contact Ben. We shouldn't be here more than two hours tops unless there's some issue created by the gear going back or some kind of severe weather over our return path." The unusual look on Janice's face made him add, "Nothing to worry about, nothing severe was forecasted."

"No, that's not it. I guess I thought we would have a few more hours on the station, you know, to wonder around, experience the station's ambiance," she begged.

"Ambiance? This isn't a vacation flight. Sorry, E3 is due for some scheduled maintenance, and they want her back as soon as possible. We have two short re-entry windows that will save fuel. Everything to the bottom line, remember?"

Janice pressed the shoulder strap latch releasing her from her cushioned cockpit seat, straightened up and with wide eyes, once again looked down upon their home world.

It seems so peaceful from space. No crazy border wars could be observed. No food shortages or riots, she thought. She knew global peace was an unattainable dream, but still her secret hope for the future that she shared with very few acquaintances.

"Ten-five, there commander," she laughed right in his face with that beautiful smile.

"Wait a minute. Don't you mean ten-four?" he inquired, just now realizing that she was about to utter some smart-ass, never heard before remark.

"No -------ten-five. That's **'my'** message received, acknowledged, and about to be performed with one hundred fifty percent effort." She smiled again, knowing she suckered him into the question and he walked right into her response. "See ya in ten," and out into the main cabin she floated like a butterfly despite the fact there was quasi-normal gravity once docked.

Matt just shook his head and thought, ***that's why I want to know her better.***

"Endeavor-3 to base, Rogers here, come in please." Matt reviewed the status indicators on his main panel while he waited for a response. He thought one of the thrusters was slower to respond when he made his first course correction a few hours ago, but nothing showed abnormal on the panels or history readout.

Something to review with Ben when he comes on, he thought.

"Endeavor-3 to base, Rogers here, come in base." ***Odd, no matter where they were relative to base, the comm signals were relayed from any point in orbit. Sometimes it was a little more delayed, but not like this. Never like this. Could my comm antennae be damaged? Unlikely, but possible.***

"Endeavor to base, come in please." Nothing, no whispery static. No nothing. Matt had another thought. He rotated the channel selector to a familiar setting.

"Endeavor to PARADISE, come in please."

"PARADISE here. Why are you using the external commlink? Need I remind you when you are docked with PARADISE, the internal stationlink is clearer," barked a rough and familiar voice.

"Pavel, just checking my external comm broadcast signal. I can't seem to reach base. Can you patch me thru your comm link?"

"Commander, I'm afraid that is not going to be possible. We've been unable to reach base for the past hour. Something is strangely wrong. I'm going to ask you to please stay aboard Endeavor for a bit. I assume Steve is aboard?" Pavel asked out of politeness rather than a request for information he already knew.

"Yes, we want to begin unloading Steve, Miki and supplies within the next ten," Matt replied with nervous breaths. "Is there something wrong?"

"Yes, commander, I fear there is something terribly wrong. I'll discuss with you and Steve via commlink in fifteen minutes. Again, please do not come thru the docking ring until we have agreed it is safe to do so. We have much to discuss, Pavel out."

The commlink went silent and Matt was left with an uneasy and growing fear in his gut as he headed to the main cabin to speak with Steve, the supposed new COS. *Pavel appears to be hiding something. And why can't he reach Ben*, he wondered? *What's going on?*

PARADISE Station - Docking access way   09:34 am Nov 4

Blade had the loading cart standing by the docking station doors for the past few minutes. Ever since his mini personal status monitor told him the Endeavor had docked a few minutes ago. He requested the computer components to upgrade several new modules and the food provisions were expected, but mostly Blade was anxious to have Pavel out and the new COS in as soon as possible. He didn't personally know this Steven Holt, but everything he had read from the SSI press files and worldAccess webpage portrayed him as a competent administrator.

Of course, a dead rodent would be better than Pavel, he thought as he played the image in his head. *But his surveillance on Pavel and Sid was far from complete. He'd miss the fun he had in torturing Sid with little computer viruses and lockouts.* Still, Blade was confused by these changes. *If Sid and Pavel were replaced, there was no reason for him to be on PARADISE. No one on PARADISE, and only a handful down below, knew that little interesting fact. He wondered if the new COS was aware of that small piece of information?*

Why hasn't anyone on base contacted me about the Sid removal?

Blade pressed and re-pressed the docking ring access control. Nothing changed.

Why was it not opening? Blade mashed on the intercomm to the command center.

"Why is the docking ring not releasing? It appears to be over-ridden from main control," he uttered, frustrated whenever dealing with objects he could not personally control.

Pavel's voice came thru the commlink in a rough, but controlled beat.

"Mr. Stormecky, please move away from the docking ring and come to the main conference room at once, Pavel out." He left no room for discussion which was normal for the current COS.

Blade secured the cart via it's wheel brakes and bungeed it to the wall as a backup. As Blade was reluctantly progressing to the main conference room, wondering what his 'Pavelness' was planning, the station-wide intercom blared, "All staff; please come to the main conference room at once. We have a serious emergency requiring all departments, Pavel out."

God, I hope Sid is not behind this. Maybe I went a bit far? Naaa. This must be something else. Pavel is not going to step in for Sid at this late stage, Blade mused.

He had planned to head to his office first and reactivate Sid's logon, but rejected that thought quickly. He turned and headed to the main deck wondering, *what in hades was Pavel up to now? That crazy Russian!*

Chapter 6   Separated by Berth

<u>Endeavor-3</u> – Main Bay   09:42 am Nov 4

Ten minutes after Pavel's command to stay aboard the shuttle, the sour feeling was still burning his gut and beginning to spread over Matt's face. This was not how he wanted to appear neither to his new co-pilot nor his passengers, but his normal cheerful appearance had been sacrificed a few minutes ago. There was little time to compose his demeanor. As he entered the main bay, Matt surveyed the faces of the three SSI staff and could read the confusion, fear, and reactions that were slowly turning to frustration in all of them.

But Janice seemed just a bit steadier than the others. Another point in her favor that may count for a lot before this is over, he pondered.

"Ok, everyone. I know you have some questions, as do I. Pavel said he would contact us in the next few minutes and requested we stay aboard Endeavor until he releases the access lock. All I know at the moment is there has been little or no communication with Ben or SSI base for a while. We didn't communicate with base for at least the past hour by my reckoning."

"What's a while, Matt?" Steve questioned as he leaned back in the makeshift cushions for their meeting in the main bay. "Do you think this is a ploy by Pavel to keep us from coming onboard? Has he gone screwy? My support staff has been observing for a few days now that Pavel has been acting very strangely." After a few seconds of thought, Steve began again, "But then, -----for those who don't know him well, Pavel's normal is pretty strange."

"I'm not sure, but my guess is this is not some ploy," Matt replied. "I detected something in his voice over the comm that was not Pavel-like, normal or otherwise. All we can do for the moment is wait until he contacts us. I tried contacting base several more times, all without success. Whatever's going on, no one's talking about it, and that concerns me even more than Pavel."

Janice sat down next to Miki and said, "Gee, if only we had a campfire and could lower the lights, it would be just like camping out in the woods." She offered that Janice smile that no one could resist feeling just a bit better, no matter the dire situation. Miki nodded downward, unaware of Janice's smile and did not reply. She just continued a blank stare, without looking at anyone. Matt immediately perceived how Janice was trying to calm Miki without going overboard and once again appreciated the skill set she naturally possessed and exercised exactly when needed.

"Ok, we wait until Pavel contacts us," Steve said, with little of the emotion that was raging thru him. "There better be some valid reason behind this nonsense."

PARADISE Station – Command Center   10:10 am Nov 4

Once Sid and Laura took their seats and joined Blade and Pavel in the Command Center conference room, Pavel stood. The lights had been set brighter than anyone had recalled in the last six months. All three white boards had been erased, including the schedules and critical tasks that are never removed until completed. Everyone sensed a serious mood. Pavel pressed the comm linking the audio circuit to the docked shuttle.

"Pavel here. Do you have a clear commlink, Matt, Steve?" he asked.

"Yes, Pavel, we read you fine. Steve, Miki, and Janice, whom I don't think you have met, and I, are standing by," Matt responded.

"Very good. I had hoped to welcome you in a much more favorable manner and I look forward to meeting you in person, Miss Wells," Pavel remarked in his most formal manner. He paused for a few seconds, as if to strengthen his inner resolve and began again. "But first things first".

The elder Commander of Station addressed those in person, and the four several meters away as if he were addressing a world congress. He spoke in the quietest voice anyone had ever heard him use, since his normal voice was rough and powerful. He hoped his words were clear, evenly spaced and commanded the attention needed.

"There is an unknown virus that has been raging on Earth for more than four days. Globally, but more in Europe at first, and spreading more rapidly than anything ever seen previously. We have few key facts, but here they are. This was communicated to me from SSI and partially verified by a few radio comms still operating. The virus has less than a twenty-four hour contagion effect. It completely shuts down all internal biomed functions. The patient simply falls down dead. They are not zombies and rise again like some popular vids; they are quite dead and may be quite contagious as well, no one is sure. There has been little information because the disease strikes so fast, with little warning. Commercial travel had been immediately shutdown in all countries, including all borders, but people are moving everywhere, not only to be with loved ones, but to try and escape from everyone else. Chaos is inadequate to describe what is occurring in our countries down below. Experts have estimated there could be less than forty percent of the Earth's population left alive in approximately three months unless some miracle happens and the CDC and WorldHealth Org are saying there is no stopping this until it runs its course or a treatment can be discovered. It is affecting all ages, all races, male and female. So far, the disease does not appear to be affecting animals or spread by them. There appears to be some people who may be immune and initial reports are indicating some link to blood type "O" negative, but that has not been verified, only rumors. If you come in contact with it, you are dead within twenty-four hours and you won't know it, as there are no warning symptoms." At this, Pavel sat down in a heap, staring at the comm mic.

"I am open to discussion and questions. I will try to answer what I can," he murmured with what seemed like his last breath.

"This is unbelievable," was all Blade could utter. Laura shook her head before easing it down to her hands on top of the table. A small sigh escaped her, undetectable to those around her. Sid just stared at the wall screen while in his head, every conceivable plan he had envisioned in the last four days were all being erased, step by step He could never remember feeling so helpless and mentally lost.

This is what it feels like to be clueless; I've got to rethink everything! He thought.

"Is this the reason you are not allowing us access to the station?" Steve questioned. Matt wondered the same thought, but he could not manage his voice to pose the question. His own mind and thoughts were spinning so fast, it was like trying to grasp a phrase that you could only glimpse part of.

"Yes, I was advised by corporate, before comms were lost, to allow you to dock, but require you remain in the shuttle for twenty four hours, in case of contamination. I've been assured there is a low probability of contamination. I'm going to require thirty hours to be safe, before allowing you to come onboard to PARADISE itself. I'm sure you understand the reasoning," Pavel remarked. If there was a tone of superiority in his voice it was well masked.

"I am well aware you have enough provisions, since you have our food allotments and you should be able to bunk down for the duration, despite the cramped quarters. If you need something, even if I could provide it, the station locks will not be opened for the next twenty nine hours and ----45 minutes. If there is nothing else," he paused for several seconds, "Pavel out."

Endeavor-3 – Main Bay   10:20 am Nov 4

Matt once again looked around the main bay at the stunned faces and said, "Well, that's the name of that tune. Can't say I like it, but based on limited facts, I have to agree with it. Let's make the best of it for the short time. Remember, we have the food and the transport off this floating rock. Sooner or later, PARADISE is going to need us. If anyone feels ill or even slightly off, I need to know immediately. If what Pavel said is true, and one of us is infected, then none of us will likely be going home. But, that can't be our focus for the moment."

"Pilot Wells," Matt addressed his rookie pilot who stood immediately to attention. "You are the acting concierge for this temporary hotel. I hope you have towels, blankets and liquid refreshment for our guests. Break out any food supplies you need from the cargo bay. Just be sure to log it. Get them comfortable and meet me in the command section when done. And I'll take a ten-five on that right now," he grinned.

"Yes sir, ten-five," she gushed, happy to know her made-up command was in fact well received. She turned to see two baffled SSI staff that had no idea what they had just seen or heard from the pilots.

"Ok, let's get us settled down and as comfortable as we can in here," Janice said, as she began opening a few panels to see what supplies she could use for the next thirty some hours.

"Pilots," uttered Steve as he shrugged his shoulders and looked into the eyes of Miki.

"Pilots," she agreed quietly, not sure what else she could add or if it would make a difference. **Would she ever see or talk to Kwan again?**

At that, Steve turned and headed back toward the pilot's bay following the shuttle commander. He closed the doors to the main cabin and then stepped into the forward deck. Steve closed the inner doors as well. He opted for privacy, realizing it was not necessary to have under normal circumstances, but decided this was not one of them.

"Matt, you got a minute?" he asked as he sat back in the co-pilot's seat. A short burst of exhaustion spilled out that was not entirely physical.

"We need to make some decisions based on what we just heard. I'd like us to be on the same page if possible."

Matt turned to face the new COS, but deep down did not know if Steve would ever actually hold that position in light of recent events.

"I was thinking along those same lines. What's on your mind?" Matt asked.

"First, there are a couple of things you need to know about Pavel that I was only made aware of this morning, prior to launch. Not a serious thing if he was on his way back to base. They'll deal with him down below. But with this hell storm down there, it could be more serious if he remains onboard."

With that, Matt dropped his datapad and began to listen intently.

Chapter 7   Revelations of Ben

Shortly after Steve returned back to the main cabin to rejoin Janice and Miki, Matt sat back in his pilot's seat and peered out the shuttle's main viewport. The Earth was hanging there as beautiful as ever, rotating so slowly, he could barely perceive it, but somehow it seemed a fake. There was something that appeared different and it took a moment for him to focus on it. The lights! When the shuttle rotated into the night-side there was a noticeable lack of lights turned on down below. Usually you could determine the big cities from the light pattern alone. Matt was not sure he could still do that now.

Down below something was going on straight out of some science fiction story. Someone likely made some catastrophic mistake and now the whole world was paying the price. Just can't get my head around it. And this Pavel suspicion. How's that going to play in this screwed up mess?

Matt began to formulate some basic plans for action, both involving the shuttle and the station. *Who should he strategize with, Steve or Pavel? That's not going to go down easy,* he thought, as he began writing some notes and options to check concerning the shuttle's supplies, fuel and main power batteries.

"Base to Endeavor, come in." The sound quietly poured out the console speaker. Matt wasn't sure who was speaking due to the poor quality, and smaller size of the instrument. He quickly put on his headset and replied, "This is Endeavor, go ahead base." Matt paused and then to assure himself he had heard something repeated, "Endeavor3 here".

"Didn't you recognize my voice? You've only been gone slightly more than three hours." Ben's soft voice was now clear and a feeling of relief flooded over Matt's face.

"Ben, you dog! What's going on? Pavel told us some unbelievable story about a virus and such. Can any of that be true?"

"Not sure what Pavel told you, but more-n-likely, it's only half the story. This is bad Matt. Worse than any disease scenario anyone ever envisioned. From what I can tell, everybody wants to blame someone else, but no one seems able to do anything about it. People are dropping so fast, no amount of planning can even get started. You eight people are the safest people in the universe, providing no one on the shuttle got sick. Based strictly on timing, everyone on E3 should be ok. I can trace you and that cute co-pilot of yours for the last seventy-two hours, but neither Steve nor Miki for more than twenty-four hours. Again, I think you are all ok, but if anyone has contracted it, you're all getting it in less than twenty-four hours. Nothing can be done so far according to most medical sources."

There was a long pause with neither speaking.

"Ben, were you able to reach Karen?" Matt poised the question with all the concern he could muster in his voice.

"No. Her phone was ringing with no answer when this thing started, but lately it's been going directly to voice mail. I just tried again a few minutes ago. Greg just told me cell phone service is going down sporadically across the US. Which doesn't make sense. Those towers should work without human intervention for months or years. None of this makes the least bit of sense. The disease appears to have struck the east and west coasts about the same time yesterday, but before any warnings or precautions could be taken, people just started dropping dead in their place. With the short exposure time and universal travel, it's spreading everywhere. It appears the only people staying alive are quarantined from contact to any new people. All SSI facilities here and abroad have been in shutdown mode as soon as word managed to get out. Communication with Europe is almost nonexistent. Right now, national broadcasts are only on three domestic video channels and a dozen radio channels. Someone said it's like prehistoric times."

Ben paused to catch his breath.

"At first, corporate would not let anyone leave the base, but that wasn't going to stop people from trying to unite with their families. Calmer heads agreed to let people go, with the stipulation they cannot return to the base. Matt, we have less than a few weeks of food. Someone is going to have to go out and collect supplies and report what's going on. According to medical we have only two suits that could remotely be considered for hazardous service."

"Ben, what about us?" Matt asked with a level of desperation. "We can't stay in space forever. We have limited supplies between the station and shuttle. We might last a couple of weeks on rationing, but sooner or later we have to return to Earth somewhere."

"Have you contacted the other stations in orbit?" Ben asked.

"Pavel may have, he certainly has contacts on the Russian station MIRROR, but hasn't mentioned anything yet. I got the feeling he wasn't talking to us much until we came out of the contagion period. He said it was thirty hours. Does that sound right?"

"Ha! Pavel, you cautious Russian! Matt, contagion is less than twelve hours and death in under five or six." I have no idea what he is talking about. I'm guessing he's trying to figure out what to do and that buys him some time if anyone on the shuttle is infected. What he doesn't have an answer for is if you are infected, how is he going to get those supplies and whose going to fly the craft back to Earth? Matt, he needs you like he needs the air he's currently breathing and don't let him suggest anything that doesn't make sense. I'm trying to determine what the plan is down here and what we can do to bring you all home. Stay sharp my friend. Listen for status on the quarters. Ben out."

PARADISE Station – Computer Lab   10:57 am Nov 4

Blade toggled the comm switch when the last words of Ben Johnson had ended. It was easy for him to patch into the modulation channel when he was alerted an incoming message was targeted for the shuttle. Blade figured it would be the OPS guy, likely trying to give Matt the ground status at SSI base. The overall picture was worse than Pavel had shared. Blade wondered if Pavel knew the truth and kept some of it back or was he not totally aware? Blade was sure that Pavel kept secrets within secrets.

Pavel my dark Russian, I know some of your secrets and some of Sid's. Doesn't matter. Sounds like we're all toast. We're safe up here for now, but how long can we stay on PARADISE without renewed supplies? This isn't what I signed up for. I hate space!

Just then his comm link came active.

"Voorhies here. When is my logon going to be re-activated? I need access to the main servers to assist Pavel during this emergency." A smile etched across Blade's face, growing longer by the second.

"Well Sid my friend, that's going to take some time. I sent all your files down to base yesterday and deleted them from our main server. I can give you a 'guest' logon for now," Blade said, doing all he could to hold back a chuckle.

"You know full well a guest logon can access nothing critical on this station!" he shouted.

"Well, that's the best I can do for the time being, Stormecky out," and with that he cancelled the commlink, just as he began to hear, "Stormmmmmmm."

Awwww, did that make the Sidster mad? And why when I sent your files down to base was there almost nothing to send? What happened to all your research Sid? Where did it go?   What have you been hiding?

Chapter 8   Station To Station

Blade finished typing the last few parameters as he completed the guest logon for Sid. He was telling the truth when he said he couldn't rebuild Sid's logon the exact same way it was before he sent Sid's files downward. What he didn't reveal and wouldn't share with anyone was that he could give Sid complete access to the station's files and systems without any of those files. He just wasn't going to do it and no one was going to convince him otherwise. A computer handicapped Sid was a Sid under some control. He snapped on the commlink to the station center.

"Pavel, here is Sid's logon and access codes for the station. It's the best I can do without his original files. It's pretty limited and I'm sure he is going to bust a few brain cells. I guess you can share your access codes with him if you want, Storm out." Blade neither waited nor wanted to hear a response from Pavel since he sent the same information via voicegram thru the station system. He'll get that message either way.

Pavel will never share his access with Sid, Blade thought***, so that threat is neutralized. But Sid is still the mystery he was when I got here. If he boards that shuttle my time to discover what he has been up to is over. Who knows if anyone is left down below who cares?***

Matt was reviewing his notes with Janice regarding the status of the shuttle when the commlink came active.

"PARADISE here, is your commlink clear Matt?" Pavel's voice seemed much more in control and as forceful as Matt ever recalled.

"We read you four by four Pavel. What's up?" Matt replied.

"Is Steve with you? I intend to contact the MIRROR station in a few minutes. We need to ascertain their status and any additional information they might have. I feel that Steve should be listening or be able to ask questions as needed. Since the shuttle will likely play an important part of the discussion and logistics, I suggest you also be involved in the conference."

"I agree. I'll have Janice go and fetch Steve and we'll be ready in ten," Matt offered.

"Fine, I will contact MIRROR and then bridge you in, Pavel out."

Hmmm, Pavel rarely plays so nice. What's he up to? Matt thought. Matt turned and faced Janice.

"Ok, you heard the man's request. Bring Steve up front and I'll let him know what is about to happen. Since it won't be comfortable up here for all three of us, I want you on the commlink somewhere aft. Involve Miki if you think best. Stay on mute, don't talk or offer up anything, but listen carefully. I'm counting on your ability to discern what people mean even if they don't say it. We need to have a clearer idea of what's going on, despite what anyone offers." Matt hoped his commands didn't seem too forceful.

"Roger that," Janice said.

"What, no ten-five?" Matt asked, a little smile forming, his eyes a faint sparkle.

"I think this is a little too serious for that," Janice said almost too quickly as if she were refuting her superior.

"No, you're right, this is pretty serious. But we're a team and I'm counting on you for some serious G2," Matt offered as he looked right into those deep brown eyes.

"That's a ten-five commander," she replied with a grin, and headed aft to find Steve.

PARADISE Station – Command Center   11:38 am Nov 4

"Mr. Stormecky--------------Pavel here, would you please establish a commlink with the MIRROR Station. I need to speak with their commander. I believe her name is Annushka Rusnak."

Blade gnashed his teeth every time he heard the COS say, "Pavel here."

Who else sounds like you or would even be giving these orders! He screamed inside his head.

Blade opened the channel files of his computer console to determine the frequency of the MIRROR station. Once he found the correct codes, he typed in the numbers and opened the commlink.

"PARADISE station calling station MIRROR, please respond," Blade offered into the mic.

MIRROR Station / PARADISE Station   11:39 am Nov 4

"MIRROR responding to commlink request, please identify your person." The voice accent was heavily Russian but the English so perfect it could have been a seventh grade English teacher responding back. Blade was shocked to get a response so quickly.

"This is PARADISE station. Commander of Station Pavel Oberholtz is requesting a conference link with your station commander. At her convenience, over."

"One moment PARADISE," came thru Blade's comm.

"Commander, it is PARADISE station, just as you predicted, -------only a bit sooner than you expected," Izolda added. The comm officer nodded, acknowledging the wisdom of her station commander. The comm officer spoke in a hushed tone, as if to prevent PARADISE station from hearing her, despite the fact she toggled 'mute' on the transmit side of the link to be safe.

"Pavel must be more desperate than I anticipated. I was expecting Herr Holt to be calling. If I recall correctly he was the newly named COS a few days ago," Annushka commented.

Apparently Herr Holt has not risen to his station, she thought dryly.

"Let PARADISE know the commlink will be established at twelve-hundred hours. I want Barkov alerted and ready at my command console in five minutes," the Russian commander spoke sharply. Her mind was focused on possible strategies and needed to review them with her second in command. She didn't really trust him since he was assigned to her station, but protocol was protocol. She thought Barkov would be more comfortable on the field of battle than in their orbiting station, but she was used to managing what they gave her. *I've trained myself to be manage whoever they assign me,* she mused. *I've been managing men like Barkov for twenty some years.* A smile appeared briefly and disappeared as quickly, as she consulted her procedures manual.

MIRROR Station / PARADISE Station   12:01 pm Nov 4

"You may establish the commlink, Izolda," Annushka commanded, maintaining the precise manner MIRROR station procedures required when communicating with non-affiliated links.

"Go ahead commander, the commlink is active," Izolda stated with practiced authority.

"Pavel, this is Annushka Rusnak and Stepan Barkov, my second. Greetings." The words were polite but the coolness suggested a somewhat hesitant tone.

"What is the reason you have requested a conference link?" she asked. Her eyes made contact with Stepan to be sure he was listening as intently as she required. He knew instinctively to listen and not speak, but was poised to write a question on her commpad if necessary.

"Commander Rusnak, before we begin, may I bridge our shuttle, --------commanders Rogers and Holt? There is likely information they may ask or provide as we progress," Pavel requested. "I didn't want to presume your answer," he added.

"Agreed. But why are they not on your station, if I may ask?" Annushka inquired.

"Certainly, a part of this discussion, please stand by a moment," Pavel answered.

"Mr. Stormecky, please bridge in Endeavor," Pavel requested. Blade adjusted a comm wheel and depressed a switch.

"PARADISE to Endeavor, do you read?" Blade spoke into the audio mic.

"Endeavor 3 here, channel is clear," Matt said as he and Steve settled back into the pilot's seats. Each gave the other the "ready" nod as they prepared to learn more news, hoping it was better than what they had been hearing.

"Bridging channels now, all stations should be linked," Blade reported as he muted his audio, but was more than interested to hear how this conference might affect his actions in the next twenty four hours.

"Commander Rusnak, what status do you have regarding," Pavel began.

"Pavel, please, you may call me Annushka. We have, how do you say, many miles beneath our shoes together?" she interrupted.

"Yes of course, Annushka." Pavel seemed a bit flustered by that revelation being broadcast over the entire commlink. But he quickly pushed on lest he appear to be overly affected.

"We have been given very alarming news from our base headquarters In Texas, concerning a plague or virus that seems incredibly destructive. We are wondering what details you have learned regarding this situation? The seriousness of this event would seem to suggest a degree of cooperation to maximize our survival," Pavel finished.

"We have been given similar information, very little details," Annushka replied, she was willing to confirm anything PARADISE might know, but was not willing to reveal any new information until she had more facts. Certainly not until she ascertained what PARADISE station was seeking. Barkov gave her a confirming nod, implying this was the correct and safest tactic.

"We have been advised that a very serious plague is sweeping the main population centers across all continents. We are currently keeping the Endeavor shuttle in quarantine for twenty-four hours-------as advised," Pavel added.

"Commander Rusnak, this is Steven Holt, COS of PARADISE station. Do you have a return shuttle vehicle currently docked or expecting one in the next few days?" The question surprised Annushka. She glanced wide eyed at

Barkov for suggestions. He shook his head to confirm not to reveal that information.

"I'm sorry commander; I can't answer that question without some authorization. Why do you ask?" she queried.

"Just trying to determine what possibilities we have in getting us all safely back to ground zero," Steve replied.

"Yes of course." Annushka wanted this commlink severed as quickly as possible. She did not like mincing words with possible rivals when she had so little information.

"Pavel, I suggest we resume this communique tomorrow at the same time. This will give us time to assess our situations and confer with superiors. MIRROR out."

MIRROR Station – Command Center   12:15 pm Nov 4

Annushka turned quickly to face Stepan and asked, "Have we been able to reach anyone down below in the past three hours?"

"No commander, I will check with Izolda for the latest status, but we have not been able to contact Tyuratam Control or the shuttle Malik that launched this morning. Izolda has been ordered to monitor all Earth based communications she can reach. She believes that each hour the broadcasts are fewer and nothing but panic being reported. I have gazed out the view window several times in the past several hours. During the dark revolutions, I can no longer make out the outlines of countries or cities based on normal lighting. People are not turning on their lights or else, they are no longer even there."

Annushka leaned back in her command chair and stared at the low ceiling. Tiredness and worry oozing out of her body. Finally she eyed her command partner and issued her request.

"Order all experiments halted immediately. No one is to waste any resource related to oxygen or water. Include anything else you think necessary."

"Yes commander," Stepan replied as he headed towards the science labs.

So in addition to a human exterminating virus, we are trapped in orbit. Why didn't she listen to her father and become a doctor? Annushka reflected. Then another thought flashed into her mind. *Two commanders of PARADISE? That may provide an advantage or at least an interesting sideshow. Ahh Pavel, why did I not return your call last week? Was I fearful of our past or of our future?*

Chapter 9   Boarding Passes

While MIRROR broke their side of the commlink, PARADISE and Endeavor were still linked via the comm bridge Blade had initiated from PARADISE.

"Pavel, can we review a few things before we shut down this link?" Steve requested with the utmost in his diplomatic voice.

"I'm listening," Pavel replied, but his remark carried little interest in what Steve might have to say. Steve picked up on it immediately.

"Listen Pavel, this is no time for acts of superiority. We are in a major jam here no one has ever even contemplated. We are going to have to work together to see this thru." Steve nearly shouted, hoping the audio leveling software might lower his volume somewhat.

"Steve, I am not trying to undermine your newly appointed position. Until you come onboard, I am still the COS," Pavel relayed. Except that everyone thought he was doing exactly that.

"Speaking of coming onboard," Matt interrupted.

"I spoke with Johnson a few minutes ago and he informs me that the quarantine period is just a few hours and all of us onboard have been proximity cleared because of the launch. We request you allow us to come aboard, unload our payload, and make our next set of plans, face to face." Matt was pretty sure Pavel would not be able to detect the small lie concerning Steve and Miki's status. Pavel thought deeply for several moments.

"Very well, I shall open the docking ring. I assume you will not be taking the shuttle down as scheduled in light of the recent events?"

"Correct. One, we need more G2 from Ben. Two, we need more intel from both of the two orbiting stations. And three, we need to decide who stays up and who goes down based on the current situation. I can't confirm what payload Endeavor can handle without someone reviewing the logistics.

I think there are a dozen more issues and concerns we need to review and make decisions on. Endeavor out."

"Whew. I was not betting Pavel would relent so quickly," Steve said.

"Me neither, but he doesn't have a lot of options," Matt replied. "It's our bus or no bus back to Earth for the time being. He better learn what cooperation feels like real quick. So, you will be the new COS after all, although I'm not sure congratulations feels like it should."

"You're right about that. This is not how I planned to start my tenure, with a disaster stirring and Pavel still onboard to second guess my decisions," Steve sighed. "Well I have another surprise for Mr. Oberholtz. It only makes sense that he remains the COS of PARADISE for the time being. I'm appointing myself C O M," he joked with a smile.

"C—O---M! That sounds wimpy to me," Matt cringed, hoping he hadn't strayed too far out of bounds with the new COS.

"Well, I need to be the Commander of Mess," because that's what this has written all over it. Until that changes, Pavel can run the station while I, I mean we," he corrected, "find the optimal solution for everyone's safety."

"Roger that," Matt replied, thinking *It's hard not to like the way this guy thinks or acts.*

"I guess we should let the women know what's just occurred," Steve wondered out loud.

"Maybe, but they probably heard it all on our commlink shuttle-side. I wanted Janice to hear it live. She has the best woman's intuition I have ever experienced. There are no secrets on this bus," Matt said with some pride.

"Well, I hope that stays true," Steve murmured as he exited out the pilot's bay*.*

I hope there are no more secrets at all. Secrets are dangerous and we don't need any more danger than what we are facing now, he thought, not believing for a moment it would be the end of secrets.

PARADISE station – Command Center   12:30 pm Nov 4

"Pavel to all hands. I am releasing the docking ring for Endeavor. I have been assured they are not infected with whatever is progressing down below. Please assist our guests with unloading of supplies and hardware. I request each of you to come up with questions and recommendations for our situation. Please convene in the meal bay at seventeen hundred hours for dinner and conference. Please be prepared to provide status of supplies and consumables in each of your areas. I'm sure Mr. Holt will require this information as soon as possible, Pavel out."

Pavel toggled off the audio broadcast with a slight slam of his fist. *That's likely the last command I'll give on PARADISE,* he thought.

PARADISE station – Docking Bay   12:32 pm Nov 4

Blade unstrapped the supply cart he secured earlier and punched the docking ring release. This time it smoothly slid open and Blade practically raced thru the connecting chamber. He forgot how cold it felt here. Just then the Endeavor's shuttle docking door slid aside and the cutest female form he had seen in years smiled back at him.

"You must be Mr. Stormecky Matt keeps talking about. He says you are SSI's smartest computer jockey," Janice related matter of factly. Her bright smile continued as if it had no end.

Blade was caught off stride, he couldn't remember the last time someone complemented him about anything. He knew Matt thought highly of him, but had not really expressed any praise to his face.

"Yes, ma'am", you can call me Blade. You should have four containers of hardware for me. They should be in containers marked C1 thru C4," Blade barely said above a whisper. He was not normally this nervous around women, but this one was swirling his brain. Just then he had a wild thought.

"I'm sorry Miss Wells, but I need to see some form of ID before we can proceed with this operation." He said this with a giant grin. Janice smiled back. She pointed to her SSI ID badge.

"Well, this is the only ID I have at the moment," she said still smiling brightly, immediately perceiving that Blade was kidding.

"Works for me," Blade replied, enjoying this small banter that never happened on PARADISE station since he arrived.

At that same moment, both Sid and Laura entered the docking chamber pushing a slightly larger cart than Blade's. It appeared to be somewhat harder to roll, with Sid supplying most of the muscle. It was already loaded with lab containers.

"These are the lab experiments and results for SSI's Texas research personnel. We're ready to offload our food and medical supplies," Laura offered. "They should be in containers marked FS1 thru FS6 and a larger container with MEDICAL stamped on all four sides. Seeing the distant look on Janice's face, she added, "Oh, and sorry! Welcome aboard!"

"Miki and Steve are in the cargo bay releasing the straps on the containers. I don't think we can all fit in there, so let's take this one group at a time. We can't load any of your containers until your supplies are out of the cargo bay. Why don't you set those over to the side for now? Mr. Stormecky. Ops, I'm sorry, Blade. Let's get your cart in as close as we can and start with your supplies."

Steve popped his head thru the cargo bay access and said, "Ready for something marked Medical. Next, behind that are several containers marked FS something."

"Sorry Blade, your gear must be farther back," Janice said apologetically.

"Ok, let's get your larger cart in first," Janice pointed to Sid.

Sid was more than enthusiastic to push past Blade and easily managed to roll over his foot on purpose.

"Sorry bud, didn't see your foot there. Could you move your cart back some more?" Sid requested with a smirk only Blade could see.

"No problem, Sidneeee," Blade retorted, hoping to verbally knock Sid back a step, but Sid was already lifting the Medical container and ignoring him. After several minutes, with Steve's help, the two loaded the remaining food supply containers onto their cart. While Sid was strapping down the cart, Laura silently wandered back into the cargo bay. She spotted Miki and snuck up on her.

"Anyone here about to be engaged?" she whispered.

"You hush about that. It's still secret!" Miki snickered, as the two scientists hugged with a warm embrace.

"Well? What's the story? The rumor mill doesn't get this high," Laura added.

"Kwan and I are engaged, but we haven't told anyone or set a date either," Miki said, apprehension growing by the hour.

"Now scoot out of here and let me get these supplies unloaded. We'll have plenty of time to catch up." Laura pointed her finger at Miki, smiled, winked and headed back toward the docking ring. She saw that Sid had repositioned the containers on the cart, strapped them down and was scanning for her to assist in getting the cart rolling. Before putting human leverage to his cart, Sid turned to look at Steve directly and offered to convey a message.

"Pavel has requested after loading and some rest, we meet in the meal bay for dinner and a conference meeting at seventeen hundred hours. You good with that?"

Steve thought a moment and said, "Yep, that's a good idea. Laura, I'd appreciate it if you can accommodate Miki in your cabin for the short duration. Get her bunked down and some rest. Sid, I'd ask if you let Janice have your cabin and you, Matt and I will bunk in the shuttle. Can you work with that for a short while?"

Sid replied, "Well, there is one guest cabin not being used, it's slightly larger than the staff cabins because it has no computer desk. I'm pretty sure there are two beds in there now. Both Miki and Janice could stay in there." Steve pondered that for a moment and looked up as he made several adjustments to his thoughts.

"Fine, then Matt and I will stay in Endeavor. Laura, I need you and Miki to take blood samples from everyone who boarded Endeavor this morning. Before dinner if possible. I assume you know the blood types of everyone aboard PARADISE?" he inquired. Laura was puzzled by the request, but was willing to please the new COS, certainly for something as simple as this.

"Well, not by memory, but those records should be accessible by computer. I guess we can start as soon as these containers are stored away," Laura continued.

There was a momentary pause as everyone looked around at everyone else.

"Great, and one more thing for you, Sid. With all your contacts and relationships with the other orbiting stations, can you provide me a report with the onboard personnel and capabilities of both MIRROR and SUNSTAR?" Steve asked.

Sid looked directly at Blade and replied, "I'll try. Should be easy enough if my access has external reach like it once did." Sid knew instinctively he now had the proper leverage to get his computer access restored. That brought the knowing grin he flashed at Blade.

With that Sid and Laura pushed the loading cart out the shuttle access way. They turned the corner into PARADISE and disappeared while the squeaking cart wheels slowly diminished.

"Ok, Blade, you're up, last but not least as they say," Janice said in a sing song way. Oh wait, I'm going to need some form of identification before I can release this hardware to you." Her smile was beaming even greater.

Blade tapped his ID badge hanging on his shoulder and said, "This is all I have, ma'am."

Janice stepped closer, squinted carefully at Blade's ID badge. She scrunched her face as hard as she could.

"Hmmmm, not a very good picture. I'm going to let this slide one time," as she tried to imitate some longshoreman voice. But she couldn't hold that face or tone for long. She and Blade burst out laughing while Steve stood there with no clue what was transpiring. Steve followed Blade into the cargo bay to assist him with any heavy lifting of his hardware supplies. As they exited the access way, Steve caught Blade by the cuff.

"Blade, I'm going to ask you for the same information I asked Sid," Steve said.

Blade looked perplexed and remarked, "I don't understand, why ask me to get the same information you just asked Sid for?"

"That's the point. I want to be sure I am getting the correct information. I trust you, not Sid. If the information you both give me is the same, that's a small point in his favor. Is there something wrong with Sid's logon access?" Steve requested having observed the unfriendly facial expressions exchanged by the two crew members.

"Well, nothing that can't be altered in a few minutes," Blade replied.

"Make it happen Blade, make it happen," Steve uttered over his shoulder as he headed back into Endeavor.

Blade looked into Janice's eyes and said, "It's been a pleasure doing business with you ma'am. I hope we can continue this favorable relationship."

"I don't know, you seem pretty shady to me, we'll see," and with that Janice stepped back into the shuttle and depressed the door locking mechanism. As the door rolled into place, Blade observed the same smile that greeted him initially. It pleased him greatly.

Chapter 10   Dinner and a Dance

PARADISE station – Meal bay   17:08 pm Nov 4

The original staff of PARADISE, plus Janice and Miki were already seated in the meal bay as Steve and Matt pushed thru the access way. No one had begun eating but several had cups of coffee steaming from their hands. Miki and Laura were grinning at each other like two school girls sharing some kind of secret.

The galley contained two counters and one table that might have accommodated a staff of four or five. A make-shift table that was added permitted three more to be reasonably seated with minor discomfort. One counter contained the normal kitchen devices, microwave, toaster, some kind of mixer, but it was clear from even a cursory glance, all of the devices were permanently mounted in their present location. The second counter appeared to be for meal prep and housed two small sinks with a single hose. The chairs were magnetized unless pressed down. Then they could be moved anywhere on the magnetized floor. Once released they stayed where they were.

Pavel arose, extended his hand and said, "Welcome Steve, Matt. As you can see, we have already warmly received Miss Wells and Miss Yew. Please sit down, we'll have dinner and then clear the tables and review our situation."

"Thanks Pavel. But before we begin, I'd like to make one short announcement." Steve strolled over to the head of the table where Pavel was standing. He extended his arm over Pavel's shoulder and resumed the speech he had mentally prepared.

"During this emergency, I'm asking Pavel to remain as Commander of Station. He knows you, the operational procedures, et cetera. I don't think it's the best use of my time to come up to speed on PARADISE while I focus on this current situation. Matt, as commander of the Endeavor, and I, will coordinate whatever needs to be done to get us all down safely. So, Pavel, if you will accept, I'm requesting you to continue as COS for the time being. I'd ask that you brief me for any critical decisions, but the station operation remains yours."

"I...I...I accept of course," Pavel stammered. This clearly was not what he expected. Pavel plopped down in his seat like a king with a new crown, eyes wide and new ideas spinning wildly.

"Ok, what's for dinner?" Steve asked and sat down next to Janice who was reserving a place for him. Matt was already seated on her right. Dinner was a mixed vegetable beef stew, French bread, a dessert pudding, wine, soft drinks and coffee. The discussion was light hearted. Where were you born, where do you live, how and when did you come to SSI? All the conversations were dancing around, coming close, but never touching the fear and concern of what was happening down below. What might be happening to family and friends.

At the conclusion of the meal, the "dishes" were gathered and placed in some kind of sanitizing device Steve did not recognize. A few members got their final cup of coffee and everyone was anxious to start the briefing.

"I must say that was the best meal I ever had in space, my compliments to the chefs!" Steve began. He glanced at Janice, who made a squinty smile, and continued.

"Ok, ok, that was the 'only' meal I've had in space, but still the best one!" That broke a few smiles and the tension diminished somewhat, but certainly less than Steve had hoped.

"Pavel indicated to me that several of you have some reports to make concerning your departments. Please make them as concise and brief as possible. I am hoping to wrap this meeting up in an hour, get everyone some bunk time and refreshed for tomorrow which is likely going to be a pretty tense day. Laura, can we start with you?"

Laura began, "I'm not sure what you want to hear. I have a few experiments I can continue on or shutdown. Doesn't make much difference in the short term. We have the most medical supplies we've ever had, but I don't see how it helps with the plague down below or if anything started up here. Food resources are good. We can easily last three weeks, maybe four if we conserve and stretch. We have plenty of H2O, but please don't waste any. Fortunately none of the current experiments require much water, so that's no issue. That's about it. Miki and I completed all the blood tests you requested, I guess I'll leave that for her report," she concluded.

"Very good, Laura, one last question. Do we have anything that could be considered hazmat suits?" he asked.

"Not really, Laura replied. "But I guess our spacesuits could be considered somewhat a hazmat suit. If you're thinking about virus protection down on Earth side, we just don't know what we're up against," she concluded.

"Does everyone have a suit?" Steve asked again.

"Well, yes, it's a contract requirement with SSI for all personnel onboard the station," she replied a bit confused by his question. "In case of a station breach or need to transfer via EVA for some reason."

"I don't have one," Steve causally remarked.

"Yes, you do," Janice interrupted and explained. "Yours is currently still stored on Endeavor with the rest of your personal gear."

"Okaaaaay, I stand blatantly ignorant of that fact," Steve apologized with an embarrassed smile.

"Sid, what have you got"? All eyes rotated to the head of R&D.

"All my experimental data and test results were wrapped up several days ago and sent down below to Ripley. I don't have any technical projects on the table. I can brief you on the other orbiting stations that you requested, either now or later," Sid responded.

"Now is fine. Everyone should know all they can." Steve nodded.

Sid stood up as if to impress everyone that this was the most important information they might ever hear. It may have fooled the new members, but the PARADISE crew recognized it for what it was immediately.

"MIRROR is the largest orbiting station by far. It can easily hold ten staff. The Russians actually have three teams of five. A team stays onboard for two months and three weeks. In the fourth week, the next team arrives, they do a team review for a few days, three at most, depending on how complex the tests. Then the first team leaves and the cycle repeats in approximately three months. There is usually three admin staff, a COS, a 2nd in command, usually a computer expert and a communications officer. However, ninety percent of the time the admin staff is assisting with the experiments and the scientists are the supervisors. Probably makes for some interesting interactions. The Russians have at least four shuttles, probably five, but some like ours are used strictly for orbit research and don't dock with their station. Supply shuttles arrive as needed. There are rumors their shuttle technology is getting out of date and falling apart. Who knows how many are still capable of orbit? There is one interesting fact not widely known. MIRROR is a multi-national company, but they do not permit more than one non-Russian onboard the station at a time." Sid paused to take a breath and determine if there were any questions. He did not notice that Steve and Blade were exchanging glances. Blade had given Steve a visual high sign that what Sid was relaying was accurate, much as it ached Blade to do so. He figured he better be honest with this guy. He may have just restored the COS to Pavel, but it was clear who was the real commander.

Sid continued, "As far as SUNSTAR is concerned, that's a bit harder to nail down. As most know they rarely publicize their actual work aboard their station. No one can be sure where technology leaps come from, Earth laboratories or space. We do know their operational staff is just four members at a time. A relief shuttle is sent every month; four new staff replaces the current staff. Supplies are unloaded, technology loaded and back to Earth. Pretty routine every month. Little variation. Their own website says they have only one shuttle operating and a new one in dry dock. Speculation is that they can't make up their minds to copy SSI's shuttle technology or create their own. That's about it," Sid quietly uttered and sat back down.

"Sid, good report. That should help us tomorrow when we contact MIRROR at noon. Maybe we can get a little farther than we did today with this information in our pocket. Ok, who's next?"

"I guess I can go next," Miki offered. "Well, I originally expected to continue Sid's research, but as I just learned, he's got little going on up here. I have downloaded all of Sid's project results and research material and can continue that work if you want. As Laura said, she and I have taken the blood samples you requested. Everything's normal. This is a summary report." She held a small set of pages.

"Question. Is anyone type O-negative?" Steve asked.

Miki glanced through the report looking for the answer to his question.

"It appears------only Janice is O-negative." Seven sets of eyes fixed on the rookie co-pilot for a moment while some wondered why until they remembered Pavel's initial review of the plague.

"Blade, what's currently on your plate?" Steve renewed the discussion. Blade half stood up, placing one knee on his chair and resting on it.

"I've inventoried the comm hardware that base sent up. There's one processor missing, but not a major concern. One thing I didn't expect was a spool of network wire."

"Why the surprise?" Steve inquired.

"PARADISE is all WIFI-3. There should be no need for any network cabling. Lab-3 was designed differently from day one but no one bothered to mention it before. From the latest documentation it turns out Lab-3 is completely shielded for certain types of experiments, so it's not reachable wirelessly. Apparently Anderson figured it out the last time he was up here working in Lab-3, but never said anything to me. He must have just reported it down below. Engineering sent up the wire and station drawings to hard wire the lab back to the servers. I'm guessing that's pretty low priority for now." With that Blade sat down.

"So the processors are for the on-site servers?"

"Yep, I'd like to install them as soon as possible," Blade requested.

"Pavel, you see any issue with upgrading the computers?" Steve asked.

"Not if they are down for a short duration, unlike the last time Mr. Stormecky."

"Two hours, three max," Blade offered.

"Ok, make it happen," Steve ordered.

"Matt, what can you enlighten us on Endeavor's status or anything with base?" Matt sat up straighter after taking a final sip of coffee.

"Shuttle's in pretty good shape. She was scheduled for some routine maintenance tomorrow, but that's not going to happen. Doesn't affect any normal operation. I had one short conversation with Ben Johnson. He indicated what's happening across the country is happening at SSI's bases all over the country and abroad. Confusion, hysteria, panic. Many with families have left the base, but they are not going to be allowed to return. Ben says normal communications are sporadic, including cell phones, land lines, broadcasts. Ben's trying to get a group together to see what they can do to assist and advise us on returning. If anyone can do that, my money's on Ben. Unless there are any questions, that's about all I have."

"How much fuel does Endeavor have? I mean, if we need to assist the other stations for example?"

"I'd have to run that by Ben's team. We have more than enough fuel for reentry, but what that means for additional station docking, different payloads, et cetera, that's a fuel engineer with a computer and slide rule. Actually, if you will excuse me, I need to see if Ben's trying to contact us about now. I'll run that fuel question by him if you like?" With that; Matt rose from his chair and headed for the docking ring to Endeavor.

"Ok, is there anything else we should review tonight?" Steve asked. There were glances around the table, shrugged shoulders and patient looks on most faces.

"Ok, thanks everyone. Please try and get a good night's rest, tomorrow will likely test our stamina in more ways than one. You can and should be concerned, but don't be overly worried. We have some pretty brilliant staff here on PARADISE and down below that will be working this to get us to safety, whenever that may be. Meeting adjourned."

Miki and Janice headed out first. As they disappeared down the corridor, Miki was overheard, "I hope you remember the way to our cabin!"

Sid and Laura filed out silently, no words to anyone.

Blade stopped at the access way and said, "See ya tomorrow Commander," and headed off before anyone could identify who he had addressed the comment to. That left Steve and Pavel sitting across from each other; both disbelieving that events could have brought them together like this.

"Got anything stronger than this dinner wine?" Steve wondered aloud. "Maybe some good Russian vodka?"

"Sorry commander, I never developed a taste for Vodka. I know, I know, what kind of Russian am I? But, while in Texas, I did discover a man named Jack Daniels. I have a half bottle in my office desk. Shall we go up there for a nightcap?"

"Tempting Pavel, but I should join Matt in Endeavor if he connects up with Johnson. Let's save that until we have something to celebrate."

"Agreed----wise----wise. Steve, I appreciate allowing me to remain in charge of PARADISE, even for a short duration. That means a lot to me. I'll ensure you get all the assistance you need."

"It was the right decision Pavel. See you in the morning. Now which way is it to Endeavor, these corridors and levels all look the same?"

"Allow me to assist. Once you get the corridor colors down, it's easy to find your way. You need to go up two levels to the docking bay and storage area."

Chapter 11   Suspicions and Decisions

<u>Endeavor-3</u> – Pilot Bay   18:10 pm Nov 4

Matt settled into his pilot seat about five minutes ago and made sure the receiving commlink was active. He was supposed to hear from Ben on the quarters and he rushed back as quickly as he could. He was slightly worried he had missed too much of the PARADISE meeting and he regretted not being able to say goodnight to Janice. He assumed Steve would fill him in on anything vital.

Man, this was a day from hell he thought. He jacked in his headphone and mic almost exactly as it vibrated from incoming.

"SSI to Endeavor, please respond," came thru his headphones.

"This is Endeavor, read you base. Ben is that you, the audio is pretty staticy?"

"Staticy? Flyboy, is that even a word?" Ben's voice was clearer now.

"Ben, good to hear from you. This has been a day from H E double hockey sticks. I'm hoping you can at least close out this day with some good news."

"Sorry to disappoint you Matt, no good news here. First, more-n-half the base has left the grounds to be with family. A few have tried to return, but no dice by security at the gate. A few took two-way radios to call back with what's going on out there. No one's called back Matt. The world outside seems like a black hole. You go near it, you disappear. The only positive so far, is with the loss of so many people, our base supplies will last us a couple of months if nothing more changes. The main question on everyone's mind is, 'Can this mysterious virus float in here on the wind or does it have to walk in to infect someone?' Opinions are flowing both ways." There was an unmistakable tiredness in Ben's voice that Matt had never heard before.

"Most of the staff is staying in their own buildings. Medical found some hazmat suits in an old storage room. They use them to travel between buildings. We've got people who continue to monitor all broadcasts trying to figure what's with this plague, but no real solid data yet. We are starting to find pockets of people, both private and government who are attempting the same thing. Amazing that a disaster like this has brought everyone down to the same level. People just trying to survive. What's it like up there, over?"

"People are nervous, but pretty much acting professional. Steve Holt has got a handle on this from a management viewpoint. People appear to be accepting his lead. Will know more on that tomorrow. Even though you didn't ask, Janice is handling this remarkably well. She's a tough cookie. Ok, I'll pass some of that news on to the rest of the team," Matt said. "One last thing, is there anyone that we can run some fuel numbers by?"

"What, you going exploring or something?" Ben laughed.

"Steve requested we know what we're up against if we need to visit the other two orbiting stations."

"I think Reynolds is still here, I'll ask him to check your options. Probably have an answer in the morning, base out."

As Matt sat back, trying to process the news Ben just unloaded, Steve pushed thru into the pilot's bay. He looked at Matt, then the command console and pretty much answered the question he was about to ask.

"I missed the call from Ben? Anything positive from him?"

"Yes and no in that order, except he will get someone to review our fuel reserves for any station visits you're planning."

"I'm not planning anything; I just want to know our options if and when. My next option is to try and get some shut eye. I noticed that Miss Wells laid out some blankets and pillows for us in the main bay. I plan on putting them to good use."

"Don't expect any chocolates, this is a no frills flight," Matt chuckled.

Yeah, that's exactly what this has been, no frills, echoed in Steve's thoughts.

Chapter 12   Rest In Space

Despite the stresses on mind and body, Matt was experiencing the most peaceful dream he could remember. Not only was he piloting some kind of super shuttle, it was one he designed himself with all kinds of silly controls and monitors. He was just about to power the engines to change orbit when he was shaken. The bright light of the dream fading as a darkened shape began to fill his view. The dim light in the cabin barely identified Janice.

"Sorry commander, but there's something I need you to see," said Janice, seemingly unable to choke out the next sentence. Her eyes were close to tearing, but he could see she was struggling to hold it together.

"Commander Holt must come with us as well," she whispered.

"Ok, let me get dressed. I'll wake Steve, and we'll meet you outside the docking ring," he hoped he conveyed a reassuring tone. "It will be all right."

"No, it won't," she said, refuting his assurance and headed out the main bay.

Both Matt and Steve were dressed and reasonably presentable in the few minutes they allowed themselves before appearing at the docking ring to meet with the rookie SSI pilot.

"What's the matter Janice?"

"It's Miki. I'm pretty sure she's dead." She was finally able to utter the words she could only hear in her thoughts. "She's in our room, the guest cabin on level 4."

She wheeled around and began striding with the confused men attempting to keep pace. She led them to the access ladders that provided movement to all of PARADISE's levels. While there was an elevator on the opposite side, it was small and only used for containers that would be too bulky to try and transport by hand via the ladders. Once they reached her room, Janice halted. She did not want to go inside.

Before he entered, Steve paused and wanted to question the pilot.

"Janice, think a moment. Did Miki appear to have any markings on her body? Do you think it has anything to do with the virus?" he asked.

"No, she just appears to be sleeping. She asked me last night to wake her at 6:45 since my datapad was working and hers seemed to be damaged. She said she wanted to feel more useful and was going to make break----fast." Janice wanted to add more but she had difficulty getting more words out. Both Matt and Steve carefully lowered her to a sitting position several feet from the guest room. They stared at each other, trying to search for the right words.

"Do we go in or seal off the room, what do you think?" Matt asked.

"No possible way this is the virus," Steve replied. "But until we're sure, I'm going in alone. We need a shuttle pilot more than we need two station commanders."

"Hold on. If it is the virus, shouldn't you be in a suit with contained oxygen? Let's not make a simple mistake we can easily avoid," Matt pleaded.

"Think a moment. I'm not trying to be a hero here, but this can't be the virus. Besides if it is, Janice is infected and she already infected us. See if you can raise Laura to take care of Janice. I'm going inside and don't let anyone else in."

Matt kneeled down to face Janice, took her hand and attempted to bring her out of her semi-shock while Steve entered the guest room. Steve raised the room lighting half way from the slide switch on the wall. He observed a blanket at the foot of an empty bed which must have been Janice's. He paused and looked around the entire room for anything out of the ordinary. Immediately realizing he wouldn't know what was ordinary. Steve moved slowly, taking deliberate steps toward the single bed on the right side. Miki was lying on her back, the covers pulled up several inches below her neck. She indeed appeared to be sleeping. Steve placed his finger on her neck and verified there was no pulse. He did it once more to be sure. He noticed a small puncture, low on her neck but right at her shoulder blade. A small trace of blood was visible despite a poor attempt to wipe it clean. ***This isn't the virus; but it's something almost as dreadful.***

Several minutes later when Steve exited the guest quarters he discovered two additional staff members surrounding Matt and Janice. Laura was now kneeling and speaking quietly to Janice as she raised her to her feet.

Laura said, "I'll take her to my room and get her settled in." She placed her arm around Janice's shoulder as she led her down the corridor.

Steve looked at Matt and Sid while he mentally went thru a seemingly infinite number of questions and decisions. Finally he directed his gaze and voice at Sid.

"I assume Matt has told you what's inside? I need you to perform an autopsy on Miki. Do it here in the room, don't move her and don't let anyone else into the room. I need a diagnosis ASAP. I'm going to let Pavel know what's happened."

Sid stammered for a coherent set of words, "Wait, wait. Is this the virus?" he appealed. "I'm not really trained to do a legal autopsy."

"No, this is definitely not the virus, so nothing to worry about there. We don't have time for legality issues. Do what I ask now!" Steve bellowed. He was in no mood for questions concerning his orders.

"Matt, come with me for a moment," Steve requested as he hurriedly disappeared toward the access ladders and out of sight of anyone else. When Matt was able to catch up with him, he knew there was something Steve had not shared with the rest of them.

"Based on that look on your face, I'm guessing I'm not going to like what else you found?" Matt whispered in case anyone was within earshot.

"I'm no doctor, but I'm pretty sure Miki was offed while she was asleep."

"Smothered, like with a pillow?" Steve asked.

"No, a bit more elaborate. I think I detected a small pin prick on her lower neck where someone used a needle. The hole was small. I never would have seen it, but there was a small stain of blood that someone attempted to wipe clean, but missed part of it. Maybe if it was dark, they didn't see the small streak that was left. This is to remain between us for now. I'm heading to tell Pavel. Not sure if I will share those details even with him just yet, but I need to read his reaction." Steve took in deep breath and began anew.

"Question, is there a way to lock out shuttle access from everyone except you, me and Janice?" Steve probed.

"I think so. There is a touchpad for security, but we never use it to block access from our own station. Besides, we're normally here just a few hours and one of us usually stays onboard. No real need for security," Matt stated matter of factly.

"We're way past normal. Lock down the shuttle and gather everyone in the meal room in thirty minutes."

"Roger that." Matt replied. They headed off in different directions wondering what new challenges might bar their paths before this day ended.

PARADISE station – L3 Pavel Cabin   07:35 am Nov 5

Pavel tried rubbing his eyes to see if it would assist in focusing his vision and his thoughts. He was sitting on the edge of his bed, his spindly legs just touching the smallish carpet on the floor. Steve surveyed the room; a bit surprised at the Spartan nature the Commander of Station had infused into his room. A single bed, a desk with an embedded computer screen. A small night stand with a soft light which was the lone illumination in the room just now. A padded chair which Steve had settled into was the last piece of furniture. No pictures on the walls. The sandy color of the wall paint seemed identical to Miki's room.

I hope in the future I can do a little better than this. It projects no life, Steve thought.

"Are you sure she's dead?" Pavel finally mumbled in disbelief.

"I'm sure."

"Are you sure it's not the virus?" Pavel quizzed.

"I'm sure." Steve had reviewed the events of the early morning but it was as if Pavel did not believe what he had just explained in great detail. Perhaps the elder COS was not fully awake as he first appeared. Pavel stood up, listed slightly as he stretched, and sat back down. His eyes seemed more fully focused and alert than a few moments ago, leading to his next question.

"Are you implying her death was not natural?" At this Steve hesitated, trying to decide what information he should share with Pavel. His gut decided for him, but it went against the thoughts he had rushing to Pavel's room. This could be a major mistake, but his past with the older COS was built on some trust over the years. People do change, but not fundamentally. He wanted to trust Pavel.

"I do, and I have to assume that one of four people had a hand it. Either Laura, Sid, Blade or frankly Pavel." Steve paused. "You." Steve wanted it to sound like he placed some confidence in Pavel, but from the look on Pavel's face, he had not accomplished it.

"Plus, there are some rumors floating around inside SSI, that you have been providing industrial secrets to either the Russian consortium or the French. Can I assume someone has already spoken about it to you?"

"Yes, yes. The rumors and accusations are false of course. I have a group of fellow managers down below who are sorting thru it. They believe in me and were, prior to these recent events, trying to exonerate me. I'm confident I will be cleared, but I can reach no one at base who was working on my behalf. It has me wondering who would be trying to implicate me."

"I assume you have some plan of action?" Pavel inquired as he scratched at his beard.

"It's pretty weak, but my daddy always said, a poor plan is always better than no plan. Let's make some coffee, go over it before we meet with the others. You 'can' make coffee in here can't you?"

He stared at Pavel who was shaking his head and shrugging his shoulders.

"Great, worldwide disasters and no fresh coffee," Steve said sarcastically. "Ok, ok, before we head to the galley to meet with the others, can you access the personnel files for Sid and Laura from here?" Steve asked as he pointed to the computer display. There was something he wanted to verify.

"Of course. I can access everyone's research files as well as personnel files," Pavel replied as moved over to the desk, and powered up the monitor. The monitor screen highlighted Pavel's face in an orangey glow, but did little more to brighten the room, so Steve pressed the room light switch and the living space was bathed in a soft but shadowless light. It raised the illumination just slightly for Steve's eyes, but the Russian appreciated it.

Pavel looked up and said, "Thanks that helps immensely." Steve heard the soft clicks and clacks of the keyboard, but the screen remained largely blank with just a few characters on it. Pavel's face was slightly contorted in puzzlement.

"Apparently my logon is no longer valid," Pavel remarked as he straightened up and faced back to Steve.

"Pavel, what do you know about Blade? How long has he been on the station?" Steve was blazing through another dozen ideas, pieces of a puzzle that just wouldn't come quite together enough to give even a fuzzy picture.

"Mr. Stormecky." Pavel said it like it was a word unfit for family occasions. "He has been onboard for just over eight months and has subtracted at least a year off my life, I'm sure. He knows just how far it is to the insubordination line and then takes a step back, while gloating in your face. Of his computer skills? Everyone rates him a genius. His cooperation skills leave a lot to be desired."

"Why don't you have him replaced?"

"Steve, he doesn't report to me. He reports thru Operations. I've made several complaints in the last ninety days, all to no avail. I figured I must live with him. I'll tell you one thing, the only good feeling about leaving PARADISE, was an end to my interaction with Mr. Stormecky," Pavel added.

"Right, right. Ok, get dressed, I'll wait outside. We'll head....is it up or down to the meal bay from here?"

Pavel offered a friendly smile. "Steve, as the new Commander of Station, you really need to memorize the layout of PARADISE. Come, I'll lead the way."

Chapter 13   Breakfast of Nerds

Steve and Pavel entered the galley almost shoulder to shoulder. Pavel immediately went to his customary seat at the head of the makeshift table; but Steve remained standing in the doorway and was intently observing the staff while trying to appear casual. He noticed Matt and Janice sitting closer together than they were yesterday and he was resting his arm over hers. Her face was a bit flushed but she seemed to be regaining her composure by the minute. He knew Matt placed a lot of confidence in her, but Steve was still undecided by rookies in any position. Laura was sitting next to Janice on her left side and ready to support her as need, but Laura also had red eyes from crying. *There must be some connection there with her and Miki*, he pondered.

As he continued to scan the staff, he noticed Blade was not present.

"Good morning everyone. Has anyone seen Storm this morning?" Steve offered as he plopped down next to Matt, a little less graceful than he intended. The table was set with a stack of plates, plastic ware and napkins, but no visible signs of food save some fruit in a bowl. As Steve was about to speak again, Blade entered the galley from the other entrance.

"I've seen him and he's not a happy camper," Blade responded as he sat down in somewhat of a huff, clearly having heard Steve's question.

"What's the burr under your saddle, cowboy?" Steve asked. That remark seemed to drive a wedge into everyone's funk for a moment, as most seemed to straighten up, eyes fixed on the computer specialist.

"Well, with your permission remember, I installed the new processors last night. What should have taken me less than an hour ended up taking more than four hours. The basic server software was behaving normally, but the auxiliary processes that monitor and manage most of the station's systems were acting a bit strange and even stranger, I could not access or control them. I'm talking little things like orbital positioning, communication control, environmental life support. Oh, and a side bonus, our logons are disabled. So, what's for breakfast?"

"Hold on! You can't just paint that kind of picture and appear to walk away! What are our options?" Steve demanded as he shot out of his chair. Everyone held their breath as if Steve might actually throttle the self-proclaimed computer nerd.

"Calm down, I'm not walking anywhere." Blade smiled as he reviewed some image of walking in space in his head.

"Give me some food, one hour's rest and I'll have the servers back to square one. I could have done that this morning, but events seemed a bit crazy around here, like someone may have stopped breathing for instance? Plus, I'm certain I can figure out what was done if I can have a few more hours. I think determining that and who was behind it, is just as important as restoring the system."

Steve wanted to agree, he just didn't know the ultimate effect of rogue software running the station and the inability of human control of basic station functions.

What if the station just starting falling out of standard orbit?

"Is there a back door, or whatever it's called, to retake control of the processers?" Steve pleaded.

Hearing that, Blade displayed the most profound smile anyone ever saw on his smirking face. His dark brown eyes were practically sparkling.

"Oh, there's a back door all right. And a few side doors. Commander, this is what I get paid for. No one should even attempt to reconfigure my systems and think they can get away clean. Give me until noon and I should be able to answer all your questions." With that, Blade rose up, grabbed a banana and practically launched himself out the access way.

Sid jumped up and practically screamed, "You can't let him get away with that! We have no idea if a single word he said was the truth. He's always hiding something behind those servers!"

Steve looked at Pavel, then to Matt, and back to Pavel who shrugged his shoulders.

"As I mentioned earlier, Mr. Stormecky has the ability to raise one's blood pressure remarkably," Pavel added with a knowing smile.

At least I no longer have to deal with Mr. Stormecky on my own, Pavel thought happily, being reminded of constant episodes of technical jargon that stood between a request for simple information.

Since Steve was already standing and commanding the group's attention, he began to review the morning's events. After a quick summary and answering the few questions there were, Steve wanted to ask a few questions of his own. He directed his gaze at Sid first.

"Sid, what were you able to discover about Miki?" From his body language it was clear Sid did not want to review his findings in front of the larger group.

"Could we take this privately Commander?" Sid begged.

"Listen everyone, so I don't have to repeat this again. We are all facing the same situation here and we need to share what we know when we know it. I've found that everyone thinks about things differently and everyone's insights into a problem are invaluable. So, Mr. Voorhies, please review your findings, for everyone." Steve sat back down and opened his datapad to take any needed notes.

"Well, first." Sid stammered. It was clear he had no idea where to begin. He had no prepared notes, and he had little time to examine Miki's body, so he thought his best recourse was on the offence.

"Since I could not perform a real autopsy, for at least two or three valid reasons, all I could do was look for anything abnormal. I can confirm this was not some virus, so that concern was quickly eliminated. I pulled a small blood sample after which I remembered that was already performed earlier. That came up negative for any drugs or foreign substances. I guess my sample can be matched to Laura's earlier one for comparison, ------just in case," he added.

"We have no autopsy table to deal with fluids. There just wasn't much else I could do. Besides, we need to deal with the physical body soon; because we have no place to park a body for any length of time. We have small freezers, but nothing her size, unless you want to consider cutting her up into smaller chunks."

Sid was sorry he uttered those words the moment they escaped his lips. Both Janice and Laura looked down and Laura released a small cry.

"All right, that came out crudely, but it doesn't change the facts. Unless you are returning to base in the next six to eight hours, we'll need to eject her body into space. Plain and simple. Now if you'll excuse me for a bit, I've been standing and bending over a dead body for the last thirty minutes and I need to stretch out on a firm bed for a while." Sid did not wait for any further questions and whirled out the access way. There was a shocked silence.

Steve perceived the staff was somewhat stunned with the latest set of revelations. What they needed were tasks to take their minds off the latest news.

"Laura, would you get Miki's body prepared for----- whatever we need to do with it?"

Laura had several ideas buzz through her thoughts and spoke in a barely perceptible voice.

"We should wrap her in her bed sheets and someone will have to push her through the AAP." She said that with little emotion while being filled with a growing grief. *This was the woman I was supposed to accompany down a wedding isle as her maid of honor! This has no honor!* Screamed in her head.

Seeing the questioning look on Janice's face, but figuring that Matt knew exactly what it meant, she offered a short explanation, keying on Matt's face for confirmation. She thought it would help to get her emotions under control.

"The AAP is our alternate access port. In case anything should happen to the shuttle docking ring and access, every station is supposed to have a secondary access port to enter and exit the station. The AAP becomes important if the main access port is damaged and cannot be used. Of course the AAP requires a suit, but it's more efficient than moving the shuttle and using the main access port. Correct commander?"

"Right on all counts," Matt confirmed.

Steve approached Laura, and gently placed his hands on her shoulders. He looked directly into her eyes and asked,

"I know this is asking a lot, but can you and either Sid or Pavel prepare Miki's body and remove it via the AAP?" He waited a few seconds when she did not respond, diverting her face downward.

Pavel joined them, replaced Steve's arm with his own and spoke in a tenderly voice.

"Laura and I will handle Miki's body. As Commander of Station, I should probably say a few words over her. I'll see this is done properly, Commander." As Pavel led Laura out the galley his nod to Steve indicated this issue was being handled.

Since learning that communication with SSI base from PARADISE was currently impossible, Steve sat back down feeling somewhat defeated for the moment. Everyone was tired and probably hungry.

"Did anyone make breakfast or is there some kind of self-serve around here?"

"Miki and I were going to make scrambled eggs, but that's going to take a few minutes now," Janice whispered as she stood and shuffled over to the pantry cabinets and began opening them. Steve joined her and opened two different drawers pulling out two large round pans.

"Show me where the eggs, onions, ham and cheese is and I'll make everyone my world famous omelets," Steve announced. This was all he could immediately think of to re-focus everyone.

"And what 'world' would that be?" Janice asked with a grin just breaking through. She was searching for any distraction to alleviate the depression that was fighting for her emotions.

"Whyyyyyy, just this side of PARADISE I think, now fetch me them fixin's,-------- please!" As Steve was busy greasing up the pans, Matt stood next to him and quietly whispered in his ear.

"Just because we can't reach base from PARADISE, doesn't mean we can't from the Endeavor. We have better rates as well", he added with a smirk.

Steve nodded and whispered back, "We eat in fifteen, and we're squawking in twenty. Head back to Endeavor and get ready; we'll bring your breakfast to you."

Chapter 14   Endeavor Calling

Matt's back had begun to ache. He had been sitting in the pilot's seat nearly twenty minutes, but never before had he experienced any kind of back ache.

It must be the stress or sleeping on those damn seat pads last night, he imagined.

Matt wasn't even hungry until Steve mentioned omelets and now his stomach was growling. He was glad he thought to mention the Endeavor could still communicate with base because so far, he didn't exactly feel like he was pulling his weight and it seemed like this mess was resting solely on Steve's shoulders. He needed to pull his own weight and wanted that to start immediately.

Outside the docking ring to Endeavor, Steve and Janice stopped at the access way. Janice was carrying Matt's breakfast, but she was surprised to find the door was closed. Her confusion prompted Steve to explain.

"I asked Matt to security lock the shuttle this morning. He probably didn't have time to tell you or give you the code." Janice flipped up the security panel, tapped out four digits and the docking ring slid aside.

"Wait a minute! He already gave you the code?" Steve inquired.

"No, I don't know what override code he used. I used the master code. I've studied everything related to this shuttle, commander. That's my job," she stated matter-of-factly. Steve was beginning to understand what Matt saw in this rookie pilot as he saw her close the docking ring and followed her through the main cabin and forward into the pilot's section.

Janice handed the plate to Matt and said, "Breakfast burritos. Three dollars ninety five cents, plus tip," a smallish smirk on her countenance.

"I thought they were going to be omelets?" Matt asked a little disappointed.

"Improvising in the face of adversity is the true sign of leadership," Steve offered in a tone more suited to a professor.

"Who said that?" Matt asked knowing full well a smart response was coming.

"Steven Thomas Holt, 2032, Berlin University. Eat in two, radio in four," Steve stated with more authority than he meant, as he settled into the empty pilot's seat. After a moment, he turned toward Janice and said, "Do you mind?" pointing to the seat.

"Kinda bossy on 'our' shuttle," Janice offered rather whimsy. "I'm going aft to check thru the cargo bay, strap down the containers that we are supposed to take back to base."

"Cancel that pilot." Matt ordered. "When we leave PARADISE, we may need every available square inch of space and no unnecessary weight. Steve and I already removed all those containers last night. Camp out in the main bay and standby the commlink. I want you on this call to Ben."

"Heading to the main bay now," Janice said, acknowledging the request without any hesitation and vanished. Matt gave Janice a full minute to connect the commlink in the main bay. He toggled the commlink to activate it, and adjusted the headset mic.

"Endeavor to base, come in please."

"Endeavor to base, come in please." Matt repeated.

"This is SSI base, read you, go ahead Endeavor."

Not recognizing the voice, Matt continued. "This is Endeavor. Who am I speaking with?"

"This is Ken Brad...." The commlink went silent for several moments. Then they heard a loud clank as if something heavy was put down.

"Sorry, I accidently released the transmit button and knocked the mic over. This is Ken Bradley. I heard the commlink activate as I was passing by the office and I answered it. What's going on up there?" he asked.

"Ken, where is Ben Johnson? We need to speak with him ASAP, over." Matt did little to disguise the impatience in his voice. There was a fifteen second pause that seemed like an eternity.

"Ah-----Endeavor. Listen, Ben has been working through the night on several projects. He almost fell asleep standing up. He just sacked out in his office less than twenty minutes ago. He really needs some shuteye right now. We don't have a lot of staff left around here at ground. Probably less than thirty people out of two hundred just yesterday. If it's not immediately life threatening, I'll have him contact Endeavor in two or three hours. For some reason we have not been able to reach PARADISE since 0600. One of the things Ben has been working on. Sorry. Base out." The static sound of a deactivated link hung in the air while they were left to their thoughts. Finally Matt toggled the commlink off. Steve was the first to speak after gathering his thoughts.

"I say we emulate Ben and rest up for a couple of hours since I don't think any of us got a full night's sleep. But I recommend we stay here behind Endeavor's security."

I'm not entirely sure what's lurking on the other side of that door, but if I'm right, none of us may be safe, he wondered.

Chapter 15   Finger Pointing

<u>Endeavor-3</u> – Pilot Bay   11:05 am Nov 5

Janice was sitting in her pilot's seat for the past hour. She could not sleep and the constant roar of Matt and Steve's irregular snoring in the makeshift "bedroom" in the main bay, made it impossible to meditate in general or concentrate on the events of the last few hours. This was the only other place to comfortably rest since there was no cushions or pillows in the cargo bay. Discovering Miki was a shock. She felt somewhat embarrassed by her lack of composure, even after Steve assured her it was normal. She stared out the plexi-steel command window downward toward the Earth. Her dark thoughts moved on to her family. Her mind was rambling in multiple directions. She wondered if she would ever see her parents or brother again. She missed them more than she believed possible and wondered if they were safe or face down somewhere because of this strange virus. Her parents were likely the safest living on their North Texas ranch. They usually kept a constant watch on newscasts. Her father would take precautions, but Skitter? She laughed out loud remembering the childhood name she had given Skip when they were both in grade school. She hadn't meant it to be permanent, but Skip and the rest of the family latched on to it. It seemed to bring her and Skitter even closer together, despite an already close sibling relationship. Skitter was a day trader and made a pretty good living out of his home office, but it was located in downtown Manhattan. An early target of exposure based on what little they learned.

"SSI base to Endeavor, come in," crackled from the console speaker. Janice quickly jammed her headset on, and activated the commlink.

"Endeavor3, receiving you, over," she replied.

"This is Johnson, Miss Wells, is Matt on Endeavor or PARADISE?"

"Matt and Steve are bunked down in the main bay, but I heard someone moving about a few minutes ago. Give me two minutes and I'll have Matt on comm, over."

Janice flew out of her seat and headed towards the main bay. She nearly smashed into Matt as he was coming forward.

"Oh sorry! Glad you're up; Ben is on the commlink for you."

"I thought I heard his voice, wasn't sure if I was dreaming or not. Wake Steve and have him join me in command. You get on the commlink here," Matt said, wasting few seconds. He hustled forward, raised both arms on his command seat, and dropped in as if pushed from an unseen force. He started speaking before he had his headset on straight.

"This is Rogers on Endeavor3, go ahead Ben."

"So flyboy, I guess we both needed a few Zs. We're down to a skeleton crew here on base, but I guess Bradley told you that. I have a few trusted staff, most with no family, who have offered to assist in getting you down safely. We can't seem to raise PARADISE. What's your status?" The tiredness in his voice was unmistakable.

"Where do I start?" Matt began. As he was about to continue, Steve climbed into the co-pilot's chair.

"Steve has just joined us and I have Janice on commlink in the main bay," Matt began in earnest. "First, I should report we had a death this morning. Miki Yew. Can't really perform much of an autopsy here, but certainly not attributed to the virus. Steve suspects it was not from natural causes either. I'm afraid her body has likely been ejected from the AAP hours ago. Second, we know why PARADISE has lost communications. Stormecky installed some new hardware last night that has disrupted all control of the station. He promised he could restore the station from before the modifications, but wanted to see if he could trace the origin of the changes to the servers. Comms and control to PARADISE should be restored soon. Third, we have a scheduled conference with MIRROR at 12:00 hours. This is follow up to a previous call that yielded little but a poorly veiled level of distrust. Steve, care to add anything else?"

Steve scanned his datapad for some notes he had been making since they first were barred from boarding PARADISE.

"Yes, a few things to run by you, sir," Steve expressed.

"I am ninety nine percent certain Miki was murdered. I think I know how, but no way to verify that any longer. As to the why, I'm somewhat weak there." Steve waited a moment for any comments. Just as he was about to begin again, Ben spoke.

"Let's say for the moment you are right, who do you suspect?" Ben questioned.

"I'd say it points to Mr. Voorhies. He was being replaced by her. Maybe not such a solid reason to murder I'll admit. I asked him to perform a cursory autopsy where he should have seen what I saw on her neck, a small needle mark and some blood. Yet he said nothing. Did he miss it by accident or on purpose? Pretty weak, but I know people. I'd bet my paycheck he was responsible," Steve said emphatically.

There was silence again from the cabin and ground for most of a minute.

"What if it wasn't necessarily the person who was replacing him? What if it was what they might find out? Wouldn't she be reviewing all the latest experiments and research he had been handling?" Ben was thinking aloud. From the cargo bay commlink, Janice broke in.

"Miki showed me all the projects Sid was responsible for on her datapad yesterday afternoon when we were entering the blood test results with Laura. A few hours later her datapad malfunctions. Coincidence? Wells, over."

"Still all circumstantial, but I want a close eye kept on Sid as much as possible. I'll hint at something with Pavel, but I want to keep this among ourselves for the time being. Agreed?" Steve asked. Hearing no response, he continued.

"Moving on, Ben were you able to get any flight/fuel numbers for us?" Steve queried. Before Ben could respond there was a banging noise on the docking ring door. As Janice was in the main cabin, she simply rotated around and pressed the audio mic to the door, but could clearly see Blade shaking and looking back toward the access way.

"Blade, what's the matter?" Janice pleaded.

"I need to speak to Steve," he shouted. Janice cleared the docking ring lock and Blade stumbled into the cabin at her feet. He was on the verge of hyperventilating, so Janice held his hand and tried to calm him down.

"It's ok, breathe slowly, even breaths, in and out," Janice ordered. Blade's heaving chest slowly began to subside, but he was still unable to converse. Steve entered from the pilot's bay, saw the docking ring was open and pressed the locking membrane switch to close it.

"Ok, what's this all about?" He inquired as he looked down on Blade and Janice knelling over him.

"As soon as I could get his breathing under control, I was coming to get you. Sorry to interrupt Ben's conference, but this seems important too," she offered.

"Blade. Blade, what's up guy? Calm down and speak to me." They managed to get the computer expert to sit up. He took in a shallow breath and uttered, "Send a message to base security. Give them this code word. Caleb." With that, Blade eased back and passed out on the floor.

A code word? What in blazes is happening? Steve felt like he was on some merry-go-round and each time it came around, there was something new and dangerous.

Chapter 16   Strange Endeavor

<u>Endeavor-3</u> – Main Bay   11:15 am Nov 5

Janice looked at Steve who was staring at the human lump on the main bay floor. Steve was plotting a dozen data points in his head trying to get a pattern that would explain what just happened. ***This is getting more bizarre by the minute***.

"Ok, we need to get him up off this cold floor and onto those cushions. Get several blankets; put one under and one over him. I'm guessing he's been working all night with no sleep and likely little food or water. He's probably exhausted and dehydrated. Head to the galley and get something for him to eat, simple foods, and some OJ. Don't speak to anyone unless necessary, don't lie, but don't offer anything to cover what you are doing. We need some time and answers to questions we haven't even thought of yet."

Janice nodded intently as Steve provided his short term action plan.

"Roger that sir," she said as she dashed out the docking ring, paused only to reset the seal and disappeared into PARADISE.

"Storm. What the heck is this all about?" Steve whispered to no one who could possibly reply. He then remembered the conference link and rushed back into the command section, hoping Ben was still on the link.

"I'll send those fuel numbers to your datapad then," Steve heard as he returned the headset to rest on the back of his neck instead of on top of his head as it was designed. Matt thought it looked funny, just realizing Steve had done it before.

"What's going on back there with Janice? Who came onboard? I saw the docking ring cycle on the console," Matt requested. Steve held up his hand toward Matt indicating he wanted the mic first.

"Ben, we just boarded Mr. Stormecky. Pavel mentioned to me earlier that Blade reports to Operations. That means you, correct?" Steve inquired.

"On paper yes. I've never even spoken to him. Base security came to me about eight months ago and wanted to place this new guy on PARADISE. I couldn't argue with his qualifications, but I was not happy that he'd report to security. I wasn't even allowed to reprimand him for changes he was making to the computer systems on the station. Had to bite my tongue several times and threatened to quit if this situation wasn't resolved. Every time I complained someone higher up said it was critical to the company and would only be for another month. That was four month ago. Finally I just resigned myself to it. Why, what's he done this time, besides what Matt has already reported?"

"Not sure how to answer that, sir. Blade is currently passed out in the main bay. It appears to be exhaustion. We're getting food and liquid into him ASAP. Before he blacked out, he said to tell base security this code word. 'Caleb'. Does that make any sense to you?"

Ben paused a few seconds and said, "Nope, not to me, but maybe it means something to the security group. I've heard one or two of them are still here on base. I'll run it by them and let you know. When he wakes up, tell that computer jockey to get those station servers back up so we can communicate with PARADISE. If no one's left in security then that boy's butt belongs to me and he better straighten up soon. Ben out."

"Did I hear you say Blade came aboard?" Matt asked.

"Yep, dead to the world for the moment, but I'm pretty sure he'll be right as rain as soon as we get some food in him and a little rest won't hurt. What the heck time is it any way?" As soon as he asked, Steve vision fell on the shuttle's chronometer displaying 11:25.

"We don't have much time until the conference call with MIRROR."

"Are we really ready to verbally joust with them yet?" Matt asked.

"Not so much, but what have we got to lose? We could delay the link for another couple of hours. What do you think?" Steve offered, fishing for Matt's opinion.

"To me, it's a bit like politics. Not my strength. You seem determined to get some kind of information out of them."

"I think they are hiding something, but that's just me. I probably should speak with Pavel about the Russian commander. Sounded like he had some history with her he didn't exactly want to share. Plus, I should bring him up to speed with some of Ben's information. Not certain what to say about Storm. We can't exactly hide him on the shuttle very long."

"I'll review the fuel numbers Ben is sending and translate it into shuttle options. Should only take an hour and I'll send to your datapad," Matt added.

"Great, I'm boarding PARADISE to speak with Pavel," Steve said as he took off the headset, and stretched.

"See what you and Janice can do for Storm. We need some answers from him. I'll be back in about thirty minutes." Steve raised up his six foot frame and headed for the main bay docking ring.

"Put another quarter in the parking meter, Matt. We're not leaving here for another day or so, but you never know what security might say!" With that, Steve vanished into the main bay.

PARADISE station – Meal Bay   11:25 am Nov 5

When Janice entered the galley, she noticed Laura had already lined the counter and table with various containers of bread and soups.

"So, the women get to do the cooking on PARADISE? Does it ever change?" Janice offered the question while wondering if she could complete Steve's request without answering any difficult questions.

"No, not really. Didn't the new commander prepare his 'world famous' breakfast this morning?" Laura smiled.

"Yeah, but we still haven't located that famous world!" Janice countered as she joined in the humorous mood.

"Well, it's not as bad as it looks. I usually get here first, more as the planner of the meal and start setting up. Pavel or Sid usually come in a few minutes later and assist with preparing the meal. It's not like meals are complicated on PARADISE. I've even managed to lose a few pounds. I do insist on making the coffee. Neither of them can brew a decent cup." As Laura continued to pull containers and arrange supplies, Janice was pondering what she just learned.

"So, Blade doesn't help?" Janice inquired.

"No, never has. And he rarely eats with us either, which seems perfectly fine with Pavel and Sid. I think he's kinda funny in a certain way, but Blade keeps to himself. Out of curtesy I'll leave a sandwich or some soup on the counter. He comes in after we're gone and eats. But he always puts everything away and cleans up. That I will give him, his mother taught him well," she added.

"Pavel mentioned that you and he jettisoned Miki's body. I imagine that was hard. Are you ok?"

"I couldn't have done it without Pavel. He was strong and sweet at the same time. Said a few words of respect. I wrapped her body, but Pavel was the one who suited up and entered the AAP with her. Once open to space he gently pushed her away from the station. I cried when I saw her float away, but managed to regain my composure before Pavel returned air side. Miki and I had worked together a year ago and she was the one who recommended me for PARADISE. I know she was about to be married, but we didn't have much time to catch up." Janice waited for Laura to compose herself and continue.

"I was planning to finish up some experiments, but didn't have my heart in it for one, and wasn't sure it was important any longer, so I just crashed in my cabin until a few minutes ago."

Janice stepped in front of Laura for a moment and looked at her straight on. Eyes to eyes.

"By the way, I wanted to thank you for helping me this morning. I'm sorry I was such a space case." Both their eyes went wide and they started to giggle when they processed the comment. Ops, what a pun!" They laughed easily and a small bond grew between two persons with no common ground except to support one another.

Laura smiled in return and said, "Us girls got to stick together. I probably would have reacted the same way. If you want, I'll stay with you in the guest cabin tonight, but we're locking the doors!"

"You can say that again," Janice responded.

I'll be sleeping with one eye open and a double locked door! She thought.

Chapter 17   Gathering Storm

PARADISE station – Command Center   11:35 am Nov 5

Steve entered PARADISE's command center a few minutes later. He had hoped to travel from the Endeavor to the command center without passing by any staff members, something he didn't believe possible. For some reason, he could navigate just fine from the Endeavor. But getting back to the shuttle from PARADISE was a trial. Another mystery. He finally found Pavel at the command console, oblivious to the soft sounds of the command center and his surroundings. Now that he had a small taste of station operations, Steve was beginning to believe that the COS position on PARADISE was not the career path he desired any longer. *It sounded good several weeks ago, but now? Besides,* **there may not be any orbiting science labs much longer.**

Steve surmised from Pavel's actions he was observing video links from the experimental labs, shared community areas, the storage and docking bays. Pavel finally acknowledged Steve and motioned him closer to the main console.

"How's Mr. Stormecky?" he asked.

Reviewing all the monitors, Steve observed the main screen was focused on Endeavor's docking ring. Just then Janice came into view, carrying a basket, pressed the locking security code and waited for the door to slide by. She stepped into the shuttle and the docking ring closed behind her.

"Spying on us Pavel?" Steve questioned, not sure if he should be serious or not.

"Spying yes. On you no. I have been observing Mr. Stormecky most of the morning after breakfast. He has been behaving oddly, which for him, is normal, but somewhat curious. He was working in the computer lab for the better part of the morning, but he went on a strange errand," Pavel revealed as he turned to face the younger man.

"Oh, where did he go?" Steve tried not to appear too curious as he sat down. But internally he was deadly curious.

"He went into Lab-3 on level 5 for about ten minutes. Then he followed the corridor outside with some kind of monitoring device. Finally he continued down a level to the staff cabins for a few more minutes. Then he returned back to the computer lab."

"Just curious, what was the closest cabin he stopped at?" Steve asked.

"He went by Laura's cabin, but I'd say he spent the most time outside Sid's room. It appeared initially that he wanted to enter Mr. Voorhies' cabin, but he stopped, appeared to confirm something on the device he was carrying and then returned back to the server lab. Something on your mind, commander?" Pavel was sure there was more to the question than idle curiosity.

"A couple of things, Pavel. I'm betting before the day is over we're going to get a different insight into Blade. It may be good, it may not. Once he's rested a bit, he's got some questions to answer. I think you should be there. I'd say, come over to the Endeavor in about an hour. Second, we need to delay our conference link with the Russians for a couple of hours. Can you take care of that? By the way, what is your relationship with the Russian commander if I may ask?"

"Of course, I'll contact them immediately, since the comm servers are finally operating." Pavel paused for a moment as if remembering events he had thought long forgotten.

"I have no relationship with the Russian commander or anyone else. We were in a few college classes together. Russian history and economics, maybe another one. It was a long time ago." Steve and Pavel both seemed mired in thought from days long past. Finally Pavel looked up, sat straight in his command chair and clicked off several monitors.

"By the way the user logons are restored and I am able to access all the station functions. I just terminated a commlink with Mr. Johnson with base operations. You may commend Mr. Stormecky."

"Glad to hear that," Steve offered as he stood up. "See you on Endeavor. By the way, I'd like to walk thru the computer lab and perhaps Lab-3 if possible?"

"All the labs are currently open access to anyone. The computer lab was likely security locked by Mr. Stormecky after he left. The code is one seven one eight, green button. Comm me if you have any trouble. Meanwhile, I'll contact MIRROR and request a delay for our commlink. I'll meet you at Endeavor about twelve thirty."

PARADISE station – Voorhies cabin   11:40 am Nov 5

Sid had been balling his fists and smacking his hands for the last few minutes; unaware that he had been repeating the same thing when stressed the past few days.

This virus situation was an unknown factor in his plans. *It might be safer in space for the short term, but it was definitely getting more dangerous on PARADISE by the hour. This new COS Holt didn't seem to miss much. Not like Pavel. You could walk an elephant in front of Pavel and he'd never see it if you stroked his ego enough. Sid had hoped to stay on PARADISE for a few more months, see what he could get by with Holt, but that clearly was not possible any longer. Lucky he choose me to autopsy Miki. I was pretty careful there. He may have suspicions, but now that Pavel and Laura jettisoned Miki's body off the station, there is nothing that can tie me to her death. She should not have bragged about how well versed she was on my projects. It was a risk, but I could not chance that she might uncover some false reports. Ripley has my back Earth-side, but that blasted Stormecky handcuffed me from the servers on PARADISE. Did I cover everything?*

Sid glanced around his cabin. It appeared exactly the way it was when he first boarded SSI's station, almost a year ago. It appeared untouched as if no one had ever slept or worked here. *Safer that way. No loose ends.*

I've got to get off PARADISE, he thought. *Can't risk staying here any longer. Time to contact my fail safe. Ripley was paid to believe he was my fail safe and it had been worth the price. But he was always going to be embedded in SSI. I required someone outside that domain. Nope, my fail safe is above him. Way above him.*

Sid smirked at that thought and began to open his personal luggage. Luggage that was only hours ago, supposed to be loaded on Endeavor. ***No, that was never going to happen.*** Now Sid was positive, even if for difference reasons. He began to connect seemingly disparate pieces of personal artifacts into a sophisticated piece of electronics*. **It was time to call for assistance.***

Endeavor-3 – Main Bay   12:30 pm Nov 5

Steve was wolfing down a ham sandwich, trying to catch up with the rest of the staff relaxing in the main cabin. He had spent the last twenty minutes going thru both the computer lab and Lab-3. He shared his observations with Matt and both made notes in their datapads.

"I figured I might as well make sandwiches for all of us once I put something together for Blade," Janice explained. She had also managed to reconfigure the main cabin into a reasonably functioning meal bay/conference room.

"Excellent figuring Miss Wells," Steve commended her as he finished the last bite of sandwich. Everyone else had finished minutes ago and only Matt and Janice were still nursing small cups of coffee. Steve surveyed the makeshift room Janice had set up. He read the apprehension on the faces of both shuttle pilots, before finally turning to the computer wizard.

"Storm, you appear to be in better shape than the last time I saw you. You ready to explain what's going on and what does 'Caleb' mean?" Before Blade could respond, the secured docking ring buzzed. Matt was closest so he pushed the access release and seconds later Pavel entered and glanced around for a place to set his already aching and tired body. To everyone's surprise, Blade jumped up and offered his place to the aged Russian.

"Mr. Oberholtz, would you please take this seat, I'm going to be standing for some time anyway." Blade uttered the words in such a revered manner it shocked everyone, especially Pavel. He momentarily didn't know what to say. He managed a weak, "Thank you," and dropped onto the makeshift seat, his face a mass of confusion.

Blade paced a few times and was searching for the right place to begin. Not realizing the best way to start, he just blurted out, "Well to begin with, my name's not Blade Stormecky. That's a conjunction of my favorite uncle Blade and a character in a novel I cherished when I was younger. My real name is David Jepson, but I'd prefer you continue to call me Blade until this is over. Secondly, I don't work for SSI, and for the record, I hate space and space stations! I'm an independent security officer with SecTrack," he added.

"Lastly, I've completed the assignment I was hired for. I discovered the person stealing industrial secrets from SSI. The worst part is he tried covering his tracks with murder." Blade finished, finally able to share his secrets at last.

More secrets, more troubles. Will it never end? Steve thought.

Chapter 18   Storm Revealed

<u>**Endeavor-3**</u> – Main Bay   12:45 pm Nov 5

The declaration Blade just shared seemed to overwhelm most of the group and several appeared ready to ask additional questions.

"Before I continue, I need to know if everyone here is vouched for?" he demanded.

"You can consider everyone present to be vouched for," offered Steve. "Just one quick question, what is the meaning of the code word, Caleb?"

"If you know your Old Testament history, Caleb was one of the spies Joshua sent into the Promised Land. If I found my target, I was supposed to transmit the code word and base security would immediately send a shuttle and officers to handle the culprit. Once Miki was killed, I was getting afraid for my own safety."

"Ok, makes sense, continue with your story," Steve suggested.

"Believe it or not, SSI suspected both Sid and Pavel. The reason for Pavel was some of the encrypted messages flowing thru the servers appeared to be coming from an IP address from Pavel's personal workstation. This was before I was even hired. Once aboard PARADISE, I was able to trap the messages and decode them properly. I noticed they were modified to appear 'like' Pavel's IP address, but the message formats had definitely been altered and not perfectly for each field. A clear sign someone was masking their messages as if coming from a different address. If Pavel was being set up, then the likely person was my second target, Sid.

The computer supplies Endeavor brought up yielded two more critical clues. The servers were modified to shut down all communication and control of the station. I suspected sabotage and a secondary benefit might have been to eliminate Mr. Voorhies if PARADISE were lost." Everyone's mind blinked for a moment on hearing those exact words, being reminded of the famous book by Dante. Blade just paused, smirked and continued.

"I was able to determine those changes came from a computer workstation used by Mr. Ripley. His electronic fingerprints were all over the software if you know where to look. Security suspected that Sid and Ripley were working together, just not how. I replaced all his files with safe backups and restarted the servers. You probably know by now everything is back in working order." Blade needed a moment to catch his breath.

"You said there were two clues from the shuttle shipment. What was the other one?" Steve requested.

"The other one was the network cable that Operations sent up. Remember we agreed it was pretty low priority to install in Lab-3. But something just didn't seem kosher. I remembered that Ripley was always using Lab-3 when he was on PARADISE. And so does Sid. What's so special about Lab-3 that they only use 'it'? All the labs are supposed to be the same. Then we discovered that Lab-3 can't access the station's WIFI-3 signal because of the way it was engineered. Completely shielded electronically by design. It finally dawned on me, the real issue was that besides not being able to reach the local servers, no one could monitor what was happening electronically in Lab-3. So Operations sends up cable to hardwire Lab-3 to the computer lab/servers. Just so anyone in Lab-3 could download computer results right away from the lab. While I was restoring the servers I took a little recon over to Lab-3. I plugged a mini computer into the supposedly "dead" network port on the wall. This is where I was supposed to install the new cable. But the 'dead" port was already active. There already a hard wired cable installed behind the wall. I traced it back near to Sid's cabin. I wanted to search his cabin, but was running out of time. He must have a personal or mini-router/server hidden somewhere in his living space. Whenever he or Ripley needed to download SSI files they were stealing, they used their own server and created a virtual private network path thru SSI's network. Wouldn't see it if you weren't looking for it. So now I knew the who and the how. When Miki turned up cold, I figured Sid was scared she might have uncovered something he forgot, so he terminated her. I was worried he might be getting desperate and target me as well. By then I had pushed myself so far physically I was worried I might collapse on PARADISE. Worried who might find me first, and I didn't want that to be the Sidster.

"If I was Caleb," Blade paused. "PARADISE was the land I was spying on. Now that I think it through, Endeavor turns out to be my promised land."

Pavel appeared to be slightly upset as he processed this news from the one person he would have rather thrown out into space than have a good morning conversation.

"Once you knew I was being framed why didn't you come to me and reveal what your mission was? I could have helped!"

"Pavel, we have a strict set of polices in my company. Remember you were still under some suspicion. I didn't have proof about Sid until today. You two seemed like old buddies here on the station. I couldn't be sure you wouldn't lean on Sid's side once things started downhill. My psyche trainers said the best way to break you down was to disrespect your authority. With Sid, it was to complicate his daily activity, which was easy by restricting his computer access and messing with his passwords. Then I was to observe who cracked first. Unfortunately for me, you both were pretty strong minded. I don't think either of you would have broken. I caught Sid sorely through investigative research. I'm sorry for the difficulties I added to your job. It's little condolence, but I was doing my job the best way I could." The aged Russian closed his eyes as he mentally processed the full extent of Blade's revelation. He remained that way for almost a minute while everyone else remained silent. Finally he addressed the group.

"I see. Well no apologies will restore those months I lost dealing with a crazy computer engineer. But thank you for sharing the details. At least my credibility has been restored with this group." Pavel smiled as he gestured around the circle.

"Apology is accepted though." The Russian extended his right hand. Blade was cautious and looked at Steve who nodded. The younger man offered his hand and they shook slowly.

"I'm guessing until this Sid trouble is resolved, we will need to keep up this uncivil charade?" Pavel wondered aloud.

"Unfortunately that would be best," Blade responded.

"Well, at least I'll know it's not personal. Steve, I should probably be getting back to the command center. I have some reports to make to base if they are still interested now that communications has been restored. With this plague, probably not, but I should at least appear to be continuing the work of PARADISE. My advice? You need to bring Laura in on this. She shouldn't be left out, especially as dangerous as Sid appears. By the way, our conference call with MIRROR is scheduled for fourteen hundred hours. We should group in PARADISE's command center." With that, Pavel pressed the docking ring panel and exited the shuttle.

"Should we disconnect this server thing so that Sid can no longer send files or messages?" Steve asked.

"No, my recommendation is to leave it alone. Whatever company secrets and files he wanted to steal has already been done. If we shut down his server, he would know for certain we are on to him," Blade explained.

"Ok, we'll follow your advice on that," Steve deferred.

Janice hopped up and addressed the group.

"If you want, I can speak with Laura. We've made some progress together and she offered to be roomies until we find our way out of this situation. I can speak with her tonight if that is acceptable?" The group looked at one another before Steve spoke up.

"Agreed, but review with her no more than she needs to know for the moment. Not that I suspect her in any way, but the less she knows about all of this, the less she can give away by words or actions. This Voorhies appears clever enough without giving him any reason to think something is going on. Anyone have anything else to add before we split up?" Blade raised his hand slightly and appeared to have a sheepish grin.

"I'd appreciate it if I could stay on Endeavor for an hour or so and rest a bit more. I'll head to the communications room and lock the doors just before the conference call. I'll be able to monitor and record everything from there," Blade added.

"Fine with me, but be sure to close the docking ring when you leave if you're the last. I'll be glad when we can call you David instead of Blade. Blade, it sounds so weapony!" Matt expressed with a grin.

"Weapony! Is that even a word?" Janice bellowed.

"What the heck! Are you taking diction lessons from Ben? He scolded me the same way just a few hours ago!"

"Before we head over to PARADISE for the conference, I want to review the shuttle fuel projections you got from Johnson," Steve requested.

Matt pointed to the pilot's bay and offered, "All the raw data and my analysis are on my datapad. We can review it right now if you want?" With that, Steve followed Matt into the forward section and secured the door panel.

"I'm going to find Laura and stay near her for the rest of the day," Janice offered to Blade who was the only one still present.

"You can stay here as long as you need to. Juice and rolls are in that container. Just be sure to close the docking ring when you leave. Steve wants the shuttle locked up at all times. See you at dinner?" she inquired.

"You saving a place?"

"I might," she offered over her shoulder slapping the security release on the docking ring.

"Then I might." Blade was about to add something else, but Janice was already out the docking ring and sprinting down the corridor. Blade's vision was fixed on her until she disappeared.

I'd sit any place you were saving, he thought. ***Any place at all.***

Chapter 19   Russian Request

Matt reviewed the fuel projections and recommendations Ben had provided about using the shuttle for possible trips to the two orbiting stations. There was enough fuel for a single trip to either station and one reentry.

"Ok, net this out for me….we can rendezvous with either MIRROR or SUNSTAR but not both, plus a return trip to Earth? What about passenger or supply weights?" Steve heard what Matt had reviewed, but needed to sound it out for himself. A dozen different possibilities were streaming thru his thought processes.

Matt re-affirmed his initial findings. "According to Ben, we need to be careful. Maybe, maybe we can try to reach both stations, but Ben advises against both. Plus if there are any docking difficulties, it may result in not bringing the full complement of staff back on reentry. Heck, Ben doesn't want us visiting any station and to return to SSI in the next few days. He's been trying to determine the safest landing zone," Matt said.

"So, what do you think? You're the commander of the shuttle. I have no authority to press you into anything you don't want to try," Steve explained.

"My initial feelings are to get our people down as soon as possible. I'm not sure what your motives are concerning the other stations," Matt inquired. Steve stretched his shoulders and let out a soft sigh. The weight of the past day seemed to rest solely on his shoulders. He tried to find the right words that might make sense for a larger cause.

"Space is kinda like the ocean. Sailors have a kinship for other sailors no matter what country they are from or what flag they sail under. They believe deep down that everyone is battling the sea first and are usually willing to help another ship in distress. It's been that way ever since the first boat with a sail left a sandy shore. Space is somewhat the same for me. Stations and shuttles are just ships sailing the oceans miles above the watery ones. I'm betting that neither of those stations has a certain path to Earth, no matter what political or company policy they are hiding behind. I just have a problem with leaving anyone in space that we might be able to save. There are theories that we all came from the sea, and there are theories we all came from space. Either way, it seems we've formed a deeper kinship for one another in those environments. With that, I'll climb down off my soap box," Steve finished with a grin.

"Well, I admire your thinking. I'm willing to fly this bus to one of those stations for now. I'd have to be convinced one hundred percent we can dock with both and get everyone down safely. Remember, everyone you add to the shuttle affects the weight and thus the fuel. I'm not playing Russian or Japanese roulette with fuel to get us down safely, but I am willing to listen to options," Matt finished.

"Commander, I can't reasonably ask any more than that, and I appreciate your candor. Easier to plan when you know where you stand. We probably need to head over to PARADISE for the conference link. It should be starting in a few."

With that, they both closed their datapads and headed for PARADISE's command conference room. At the docking ring, Matt said, "Steve, after you, since you know your way around PARADISE so well!" Matt teased.

"Pilots!" Matt sighed as he shook his head and proceeded down the corridor, hoping it was the correct direction.

PARADISE station – Command Center   1:55 pm Nov 5

When Pavel saw Matt and Steve enter into the Command Center, he rose up in his chair and pointed to the two closest chairs to the commlink speaker.

"Welcome, welcome, Steve, Matt. Coffee is there, cream and sugar there," as Pavel pointed to the adjacent table. Mr. Stormecky will bridge on MIRROR in a few minutes. Do you want him to bridge in the shuttle as well?" Pavel asked.

"No, that won't be necessary. Just us for this one," Steve replied as he poured coffee for himself and Matt. The command conference room seemed larger than it needed to be with so few staff on at any one time. The table appeared to be white oak, but a careful examination proved it to be synthetic plastic and extremely light weight. This was only the second room with a transparent section to view Earth-side. The sight was still inspiring no matter how often one viewed it.

"Very good. Steve if I may ask, what is it you are seeking on this conference?"

"I think I just answered that for Matt a few minutes ago. I just want to know if they think they will need our assistance in returning to Earth. Nothing really more than that. Do you think the Russian commander, what was her name, Rusnak? Will she at least reply truthfully to that question?"

"I don't know. I see no reason for her to withhold any general status with us. You know us Russians; we keep things close to the vest. We shall see," Pavel offered, hoping his words conveyed a more positive tone than his thoughts were at the moment. Any additional thoughts were interrupted by the commlink and Blade's voice.

"MIRROR station has requested the commlink. Bridging them in now------go ahead MIRROR."

"PARADISE station, this is MIRROR, Commander Rusnak," poured out the commlink. The voice was familiar, but the tiredness was all too evident. ***Things were not going well on the Russian station***, Steve surmised to himself.

"Commander Rusnak, how are you this day?" Pavel began.

"Well Pavel. Especially looking down on our motherland. Barkov says there are fewer lights on at night, but it still seems peaceful, despite the fear and danger that appears to be, how you say, running in muck?"

"Running amuck, yes it means, out of control. Sitting with me is the Endeavor Commander Matt Rogers, and Commander Steve Holt who would like to review your current status."

"Agreed. But Pavel, before Mr. Holt begins, I need to ask a favor of PARADISE. One of our scientists has had a small accident. She slipped and fell and apparently struck her head. We found her just an hour ago. She has a large cut on her arm which we have managed to stop the bleeding, but she will need stiches. She is in a coma that we would like your doctor, Mr. Voorhies, to observe and make any medical decisions he thinks required. I'm sorry to borrow your only doctor but the woman's condition could be critical," she finished.

Steve immediate hit the mute button on the commlink and said, "Let me take this for a moment." He depressed the mute again to activate his audio.

"Commander Rusnak. We have in fact 'two' qualified doctors onboard; Miss Yew is well trained for the emergency that you are describing, but if you insist on Mr. Voorhies, then we will certainly consider sharing him."

"Oh, I thought Miss Yew was-------" The commlink went dead. A few moments passed as the three men stared at each other, looks of confusion mirrored in their faces. The commlink buzzed active again.

"Sorry Commanders, my apology. The commlink faded for a moment. Of course, Miss Yew would be acceptable if you think best. How soon can you shuttle her over to MIRROR?"

Steve looked at Matt and shrugged his shoulders and gestured for Matt to answer.

"We could have a rendezvous with MIRROR in less than three hours". The flight time should not take long. Probably longer to go thru systems and status checks on the shuttle. I can initiate pre-flight systems check now if everyone agrees?" Matt asked.

"Commander Rogers that is excellent news. I will pass that information on to the rest of the staff, to minimize their worry. We will have everything prepared for Miss Yew's visit."

"Well, we'll make the decision on which doctor is best suited for your emergency at the last moment, but be assured, some doctor will be making a house call in a few hours," Steve replied.

"House call? What does this phrase mean?" offered the confused Russian.

"Oh, sorry. It means a doctor visiting your place, your station. Matt, go ahead and start making shuttle preparations," Steve requested with several nods.

Matt headed out the command center and gave the two men a 'thumbs up' sign. Steve partially returned the thumbs up, only his thumb was pointing at himself. Matt was uncertain what that meant, but surmised that he should not launch without speaking with Steve first.

"Commander Rusnak. May I pose three questions?"

"Go ahead commander," the Russian returned.

"Number one, are you in contact with your ground control? Second, are you expecting a rescue shuttle in the near term? Lastly, are you in need of any supplies we may be able to offer?" With those questions finally asked, Steve sat back in his chair and was ready to key in notes on his datapad based on the Russian's response. Expecting a slight delay, Steve was surprised at how quickly the Russian commander began to answer his questions.

"I thank you commander for your concerns, but be assured, we have all the needed supplies to last us several months. We do not have a scheduled, as you say, 'rescue shuttle', but we expect one long before we run out of needed supplies. Communication with our launch base has been minimal. However, we are aware of the details of the situation going on below. Our more learned scientists aboard are recommending we stay on MIRROR as long as possible. This provides more time to understand the disease, how it spreads and what precautions might be available to take. Is this not the plan for PARADISE?" the Russian commander countered back.

"Our supplies will not last for months. We estimate three to four weeks maximum. We will then have to return to Earth whether we want to or not. It may be possible, depending on fuel reserves to take one or two of your staff down early, if they desire of course," Steve offered.

"Thank you commander. I will pass on this option to the scientists. Of course my command staff must stay aboard MIRROR. If there is nothing else, we will await your doctor in the next few hours. MIRROR out." The commlink went silent.

Steve and Pavel stared at each other for a few moments, each deep in their own thoughts, processing the words and tone of the commlink that had just ended.

Steve began, "You must have caught the mistake Rusnak made concerning Miki?"

"Yes, she was acting as if only Sid was available. She knew Miki was already dead. This implies Sid must have contacted them and requested asylum on their station," Pavel remarked.

"My thoughts as well. I say we deliver Mr. Voorhies to MIRROR and leave him there. That solves one major issue on this station. With everything that is going on below, I doubt that SSI's security cares this little corporate spy got away," Steve pondered. "On the other hand, there is the issue of a murder."

"Impossible to prove at this point, but I agree with the rest of your thinking. If the need ever arrives, I will back you on this decision. One question, what was the hand signal you gave commander Rogers, your thumbs pointing to yourself?" asked Pavel.

"Well I wasn't sure he would get it, but from the look on his face, I'm pretty sure he did. It meant, he was not to launch Endeavor without me aboard," Steve replied.

"Why? What would you be doing on this mission?" Pavel asked with a look of disbelief. Steve stood up, closed his datapad and headed out the accessway. He took one last sip of cold coffee and set the cup back down on the table.

"I just demoted myself to security. That's the second demotion in one day. At this rate I may soon be the janitor," Steve said as he exited the command center and began his jaunt to Endeavor. Stopping after several steps, he returned to the entrance of the command center and peaked directly at Pavel.

"Pavel, is there any kind of weapon or gun on PARADISE?"

"I'm sorry Steve that is against company policy to have such a thing. The most dangerous weapon we might have is a small lab knife," Pavel offered.

"The most dangerous weapon on PARADISE is the heart of a man," Steve reminded the COS. The Russian nodded in mutual agreement.

"Pavel, please put out an all station broadcast for Janice to return to the Endeavor immediately. I suggest you contact Mr. Voorhies and let him know a doctor was requested for MIRROR and he needs to report to Endeavor within the next thirty minutes. Don't be surprised if he's not surprised," he added, and disappeared once again.

MIRROR Station – Command Center   02:25 pm Nov 5

Commander Rusnak toggled the commlink from her control panel and breathed a sigh of extreme tiredness. She had not slept in over thirty hours even though she had lain down in her cabin for a few hours. She pounded her fist knowing she had made a mistake referring to the 'only' doctor. Stepan had immediately muted MIRROR's side of the commlink before any further part of her sentence was heard, but the damage was likely already done. **Commander Holt is no fool**, she thought, thankful for Stepan's quick reaction. She turned to her second in command. He was not smiling.

"As you heard, a doctor, likely Mr. Voorhies, will be joining us in a few hours. In case anyone from PARADISE should want to come aboard as well, we need to create the deception of an injured person. Have Tatiana ready on a bunk, covered with some bloodied towel. Just in case. Once Voorhies comes aboard, request their shuttle to leave at once," she commanded. Barkov stood straight, legs apart, arms at his sides. He didn't need his arms to accentuate a sentence since his voice was so precise and military ordered. He morphed into this pose so often lately. It made the scientists nervous.

"I'm sorry commander, but I have different plans concerning SSI's shuttle," he began. "I will take control of the shuttle in case shuttle Nikon cannot be repaired in time. I am sure either I or Verusha can pilot this machine, having trained many days and hours on this very model in simulations. It's little different from our launch vehicle. You know I pilot space bound and Verusha pilots Earth bound. It is the only joy of our responsibilities on MIRROR," he finished.

"Very well, please record those plans into the station log. I will not be responsible for this course of action," she admonished him.

"Already recorded commander. I will handle this alone. There is no need for any patient deception either. Tatiana can continue with her experiments. The pilots will not come aboard alive," he concluded, and exited her command station with a triumphant strut.

Needless death on Earth and needless death in space. There appears to be no difference, she thought. **No difference in the hearts of men.**

PARADISE Station – Computer Lab   02:27 pm Nov 5

Steve knocked on the computer lab door; unsure if Blade/David was here or in his personal cabin, but guessing this was the most likely. He heard a barely perceptible click, followed by a "come in". He opened the door and stepped in. The room was extremely dark, but once his eyes got used to it, he could identify most of the equipment, even if he didn't know what their functions were.

"I got your message on my datapad, what gives?" Steve requested as he continued to scan around in the computer center, still wondering what most of the flashing and blinking lights signified.

"I bridged in to your commlink with the Russian station. Heard everything. Nice catch on the Russian commander's mistake. Further evidence Sid is in communication with them somehow. You planning on going there as well?" the computer expert asked.

"I was planning on it------yes. I'd feel better if I had some weapon, but Pavel tells me no such thing is permitted on Paradise," Steve replied.

Blade nodded and reviewed some long ago thoughts. Having reached a decision, he opened the bottom drawer of his computer desk, and slid his hand underneath the bottom of the second drawer. He withdrew a nine millimeter handgun and handed it to the commander. As Steve rotated the handgun, his eyes grew larger, unsure if his vision was deceiving him.

"Pavel said this was not permitted. You smuggled this up here?" Steve was still a bit shocked.

"Didn't need to smuggle anything. I'm in security remember? Try to bring it back, it's still registered to me," Blade said, not sure if the events transpiring below would require records any longer.

"Oh and one last thing. If you must fire it, try to hit your target. Random shots tend to hit things that are critical in space," he added.

I don't intend to fire anything as long as no one forces me to, Steve thought as he jogged to the upper level and the docking ring to the Endeavor.

Chapter 20   Endeavor Prepared

Matt was just completing the pre-flight system checks when his co-pilot burst into the pilot's compartment. It startled him momentarily even though he was expecting her.

"We're launching?" was all she could utter until her breathing settled down from the non-stop trek she made from her temporary cabin to the Endeavor. She was hesitant to leave Laura, but the summons sounded serious.

"Yes, we're taking Sid to the MIRROR station, and with any luck, we're leaving him there. He can be their problem. That's no repeat information, pilot," Matt added.

"Roger that. Is there anything else on the pre-flight you need? I'm anxious to be off PARADISE; even if it's only for a few hours," Janice offered quietly as if it might be against some company policy. She just realized that only a day ago she had wanted to spend more time on PARADISE. But not like this mess. Matt faced his co-pilot, looked directly into those bottomless eyes and with his most sincere tone, tried to reassure her.

"I hear. This has been some screwed up mission for a first time pilot, but you've performed with exceptional service. At least that's what I'll put in the log, if I ever get to document this mission." She stared at Matt with that unfathomable look that could mean almost anything. They both were thinking of leaning in and trying that first kiss, but were afraid for a number of reasons. Instead they smiled back at each other, the moment passed, but the seed was definitely planted.

"Please take your seat, pilot." Matt motioned to the empty seat next to him. Janice hopped into it and began latching her shoulder straps and readjusting the seat since Steve had been sitting in it the last few times and it was adjusted for someone much taller.

Matt referred to me as 'pilot', she finally realized as a minuscule smile spread out, her face beginning to brighten. The tension of the situation lessened somewhat.

Five minutes later Steve popped his head into the Endeavor's pilot compartment.

"How soon are you ready for this circus event?" he queried both the shuttle pilots.

Matt spoke since he had a better read on where in the pre-flight check list they were.

"Ten minutes, -----fifteen max. I want to review the flight path with Ben and double check a few readings." Matt paused a moment.

"Since Janice is already strapped in and assisting me in pre-flight, I'd appreciate it if you could ensure Sid is secure in his seat when he comes aboard."

"No can do, commander," Steve replied. The response shocked the pilots as they both turned, expecting some kind of weird excuse.

"I know there's no passenger seat in the cargo bay, but I'll secure myself somehow. No one else is to know I'm onboard. I have to get back there before 'doctor' Voorhies gets here. Sid has been on SSI's shuttles enough times to know how to secure himself," Steve added. Having made his declaration, Steve turned and headed back to the cargo bay. Janice glanced at Matt for an explanation, but got the proverbial shrugged shoulders.

PARADISE Station – L4 Voorhies cabin   3:24 pm Nov 5

Sid was sitting at his computer station when the commlink from Pavel revealed he was to be shuttled to MIRROR to attend to some medical emergency. He was positive there was no medical issue, but understood the logic they must have used to request his presence. He never trusted MIRROR's COS, but had sufficient dealings with Barkov that his request for asylum on MIRROR would be honored. That he might have more industrial secrets was a sure hook Barkov could not resist. Sid still had more information to trade; unfortunately he did not have it with him. It was all sent down to Ripley two days ago. As long as Ripley has kept a low profile, we can barter that information into a secure future, despite what maybe commencing down below. Sid gathered up a small medical bag to complete the ruse. He placed some instruments, bandages, a few medicine bottles and placed them on top of some 'personal' items he was taking to MIRROR. He was positive he would not be returning to PARADISE again. One last look around his cabin confirmed he had what he needed and no longer cared what he would leave behind. As he exited his room he did not lock it, in fact, he did not even close the door. **Thank you SSI. You made me a pretty penny,** he mused as he headed toward the accessway for the Endeavor.

Endeavor-3 – Pilots Bay   3:31 pm Nov 5

"Pre-flight complete. Ready to release from PARADISE. Did Sid ever get onboard?" Matt asked Janice.

"If so, he didn't announce himself. I'll go back and check," she answered as she released her shoulder straps and exited the pilot's bay. She entered the main bay just as Sid was entering thru the accessway. Since it was open, Janice assumed Steve had left it that way for Sid to enter.

"I would say you are just in time, but since you are the reason for this mission we would have waited. Sit here please." Janice pointed to the first passenger seat that secured Steve Holt just the day before. **It seemed like a week ago,** Janice thought to herself.

"If your bag fits behind your feet, you can store it there or I need to place it in this side storage compartment."

"It fits under my seat just fine. I believe I know how to latch these seat belts and shoulder harnesses," he offered. "But you'll need to double check them per procedure," he rattled off as if mocking the safety procedures.

"Of course, --------looks ok, nice and tight, but you still can breathe? Once I seal the accessway and depressurize the lock, we are ready to release from PARADISE," Janice commented ignoring the veiled rudeness her passenger displayed. She depressed the accessway cycle lock, checked the illuminated status indicators, gave Sid a 'thumbs up' and returned back to the pilot's bay.

"Sid is harnessed in, accessway closed, locked and status green for release.

Matt got on the shuttle comm and announced, "We are ready to release from PARADISE in the next minute."

Matt remembered Steve's words about this mission being a circus event. He smiled a little as the words from his grandfather came to mind when he reviewed the latest local or national political events. ***The BIG TOP may not always be where the action is, but it always has the biggest spotlight. For the next few hours, that spotlight is on Janice and me. Please don't let me make a mistake I can't live with.*** With that thought filed away, Matt reviewed his instrumentation panels one last time. Having prepared the shuttle for launch, he now needed to prepare himself.

Chapter 21   Russian Rendezvous

Endeavor-3 – Pilots Bay   3:44 pm Nov 5

"Pre-flight checks complete, ready for detach. Did you check the flight path with Ben?" Janice requested, still keeping her eyes on the three most critical sensors and gages.

"Yes and it's a good thing. The listed orbit for MIRROR in the handbook was out of date. Apparently when they made the latest upgrade to the station they needed to push the orbit out because of the increase in mass. Tracking orbit is programmed and confirmed now," Matt responded, clearly back in his comfort zone and not like a useless tool he felt aboard PARADISE. Janice noticed the change immediately from his voice alone.

"Release docking clamps," Matt ordered.

"Docking clamps released," Janice responded after depressing the CL-ST toggle. The metallic release sound vibrated thru the cabin and Janice was sure throughout the spacecraft.

"Starboard thrusters one quarter."

"Clearing PARADISE------PARADISE clear," Janice relayed as she viewed the starboard camera and proximity screen.

"Aft thrusters one quarter until we clear PARADISE by one K."

"Point.......two....point........three....point.....five...point eight...passing one kilometer now."

"Autopilot engaged. Endeavor can maneuver us to within MIRROR's orbit and I'll handle the dock manually. Hopefully their accessway port is still standard," Matt offered in his usual cool and professional voice. "Otherwise you may have to climb into a suit and help our passenger over to the station," he kidded.

"Hey, that might be fun," she joked back. "Plus, I think I get extra pay for spacewalks!" Now she was really beaming.

Both pilots were managing the craft from a visual manner of gages and panels as well as manually adjusting a dozen switches and spin wheels. Janice could feel tiny thruster adjustments the autopilot was using to course correct. As she viewed one screen and made a few mental calculations, she looked up.

"Wait a minute, this appears that we are going in the opposite direction from MIRROR?" Janice remarked.

"Very good pilot, I was wondering when you would notice that important piece of data. Now tell me, why this trajectory is best?" Matt requested. Janice was silent for several seconds, nervous that not providing the correct answer would make her look less skilled in flight trajectories, something she excelled at.

"Let me think. This direction is longer, but not significantly longer to make a whole lot of difference, so the extra fuel is not really a factor. I'm not finding a reason for this flight path," she finally omitted.

"What's the first thing we must we do when we get to MIRROR?" Matt hinted.

"Besides dock?" she wondered aloud.

"Not besides dock, the first thing is we dock," Matt began his teaching lesson.

"What side does Endeavor dock?"

"Starboard side," she offered weakly, her mind racing ahead.

"If we reach MIRROR from the shortest route, what side of Endeavor would be facing their accessway port?"

"Our port side"

"And what would we have to do to dock?" Matt asked, knowing the whole solution was now before her.

"We'd have to thrust the shuttle completely around, which takes a lot skill and -------- fuel," she finally saw the reasoning. "Going this direction, we're already using the Earth rotation and glide. Once we reach MIRROR, docking should be relatively simple."

"Very good. That is standard docking 101. Always plan for the direction of your spacecraft and the orientation of the docking platform. Once you screw up, you never forget it again," he added. Janice contemplated a thought before she spoke.

"Oh, and did 'you' screw up one time commander?" Janice asked in her sweetest voice.

"That pilot, is 'classified' information, subject to internal policies," he shot back at her.

"Right, but I'm guessing the short answer is-----yes!" Janice was enjoying raking her senior pilot over the verbal hot coals, if even for a second.

Matt got serious for a moment; he thought to use this discussion as a teaching tool.

"Any mistakes in which you get to live thru, are teaching events. Sometimes they are the most important mistakes you can make." Matt nodded. Janice nodded back. There was no further need for any more teaching words.

"Contact MIRROR and alert them we are on glide path to their station, ETA approximately twenty five minutes," Matt requested. Janice sprang into action and began to set up the commlink.

MIRROR Station – Command Center   03:55 pm Nov 5

Stepan began to address his commander with the shuttle status information she probably already received from Izolda.

"SSI's shuttle will be here momentarily. I will board the craft under the guise of a welcoming committee. Once I observe what the situation is, I will take the necessary action. The shuttle will be ours and we can leave this…this… place," his discomfort barely under control.

"Ahh Stepan. At last your feelings for our station are exposed. Of course I have always known, I was just never sure why. You have always hated this place. Why you return to MIRROR with us is a mystery I've tried to unravel for months," Annushka offered.

"I have had my reasons. With this plague, I fear those reasons are no longer valid. I wish to leave this metallic hell hole and stand in the waves of my beloved home on the Baltic Sea. With my family. Perhaps that is not possible, but dreaming of it from here is no longer acceptable. I will contact you when it is done." Stepan turned in a military manner that no one had used in years except him. He exited her command station and for the first time in her orbiting career, she wondered who really was the COS of MIRROR?

What Stepan is planning is not right, but I'm not sure what is really right. My babushka! You tried to teach me the simple lessons of a good life and I ignored you so many times! Did any of your teachings stay with me?

PARADISE Station – Command Center   4:01 pm Nov 5

Laura had entered the command center and strode over to where Pavel was seated. He was so entrenched in the figures on his monitor he was unaware she had entered the room until she laid her hand on his shoulder while placing some tea on his desk. He was momentarily startled, but did not look up. He knew she had set a cup on the desk from the sound and vibration.

"Thank you Laura. I appreciate the gesture. I was going to take a break here in a few minutes and start some dinner planning. I'm not sure when the Endeavor will return, but we should have something ready for them, no?" Pavel spoke with a softness that surprised him. The reaction on her face pleased him. *Why had I not used softer words with my staff before? It is what Steve does so easily. Have I learned too late?*

"What's going to happen to Sid?" she asked.

"The plan is to hopefully leave him on MIRROR, but anything can happen. Don't worry, if Mr. Voorhies returns to PARADISE, we will deal with him. He will not harm anyone again. You have my word."

It will be best if Mr. Voorhies never sets foot on PARADISE again, Pavel thought.

Endeavor-3 – Pilots Bay   4:09 pm Nov 5

"There's the station, one kilometer away. E3 on track," Janice announced as was her primary function when docking. Matt had taken Endeavor off autopilot several minutes ago and was now just feeling the proper thrust of the engines.

"Slow to point two."

"Slowing to point two", Janice repeated, verifying by her screen monitor.

"Slow to point one."

"Slowing to point one," Janice verified.

"Aft engine off."

"Aft engine is off."

"Forward brake, one burst," Matt relayed.

"One burst."

"Forward brake, one burst," Matt repeated.

"One burst."

The Endeavor was floating like a white magical bird within two meters of the Russian station.

"Ok, Miss Wells. How do we line up with their docking ring?" Matt requested.

"Visual is ok, the mag clamps will align us once we are close. Just need that last port thrust to nudge us over. Standing by mag clamps."

"Port thrust, one quarter burst," Matt said as he depressed the thruster gun."

"Two meters and closing. One meter------mag clamps engaged." Several panel lights went from yellow to green as expected.

"We are docked and locked. Although I never would have believed we'd be doing this on a competing station," Janice mused.

As they both were engaged in the lockdown procedures, Matt began, "It's not so cutthroat as the newsvids would lead you to believe. I've actually docked on MIRROR twice in the past four years. Usually to drop off some critical supply or tool, when our shuttle was ready to launch and theirs was unavailable. Their shuttle docked to PARADISE once two years ago, to deliver extra H2O when a tank experienced an external leak. We compensate each other fairly. If you can't call your neighbor in space, who can you call?" Matt finished, just realizing in his mind that sounded a whole lot similar to what Steve had just shared with him hours ago.

"Ok, let's open the docking ring and let our doctor do his duty. I'll complete the engine shutdown procedures, no telling how long we're here. Let's hope it's not too long."

Before he could look up from his screen consoles, Janice was out of her seat and heading aft to the cargo bay. He thought he heard "On it", but could not be certain.

That gal must have fairy dust in her feet, he wondered.

Endeavor-3 – Main Bay   4:19 pm Nov 5

Janice streamed into the passenger bay as Sid was just rising. He was indeed familiar with the personal safety straps and had removed them easily. Janice thought he seemed in very much a hurry to exit Endeavor. He had already toggled the accessway switch and she could hear the decompression jets balancing the pressure and alerting her that it was nearly complete.

"For future reference, please do not touch the shuttle docking controls. That's what I get paid for," Janice said, internally angry, just not showing the least sign of it.

"Of course, my apologies. Just trying to be of some service," Sid offered, but clearly in a state of near panic.

What's going on with him? Janice thought.

Once he was standing and clear of his shuttle seat, Sid reached down and withdrew a small caliber pistol from his medical bag. He wasted little time in pointing it toward the rookie pilot. "Get on the commlink and tell your fellow pilot to come to the passenger bay immediately. Tell him you have an emergency, no more, no less", Sid demanded in a voice charged with coldness and impatience. He continued to point the pistol at Janice, but his hand refused to stop shaking as if the gun was wired to some low level electrical energy.

Janice remained still, her hands to her face, eyes riveted on the weapon in Sid's hands. She tried to will her body to move but was incapable of action.

"Do it now!" Sid yelled, but at the same moment Matt pushed through the flexible door into the passenger bay. Seeing Janice rock still and Sid with some kind of revolver, a dozen different scenarios pulsed thru his head, momentarily causing him to remain silent.

"You both will exit the shuttle----now! I'm taking the Endeavor," Sid was finally able to speak in a more normal tone, regaining some composure.

"I will return it, but then, it will be on Earth and you will be on MIRROR. Wrong place, wrong time. I'd be sorry, but then, I don't think I have ever been sorry. It's not a familiar emotion for me," he boasted.

Matt put his arm around Janice, trying to assure her that things would be ok. She still could not speak or move. Her eyes continued to be fixed on the weapon in Sid's hand.

"Come on Sid, this is crazy! Who's going to pilot the shuttle, -----you?" Matt shouted. It was all he could offer for the moment. The incredulous scene had momentarily blanked his memory that somewhere back in the cargo bay was their cavalry. It just began to dawn on him.

Come on Steve, time to come to the rescue, Matt hoped.

"Put the gun down Sid." The strong voice came from behind the medical scientist and startled him. He had not anticipated there was anyone else onboard.

I'm such a fool! For the past few days I have not been thinking things through, Sid mentally chastised himself.

Steve waited a moment and then stepped forward and grasped the pistol from Sid's hand, since Sid did not respond to his demand.

"You can leave the Endeavor Mr. Voorhies, but know this. We have discovered everything you tried to cover up. Oh and Mr. Ripley? Languishing in the base jail which is far better than what I'd rather do with you. But, under the circumstances, you can stay here with your 'comrades' and hope to hell there is a shuttle headed your way." Steve surprised himself in that he had not lost his temper that had building ever since he found Miki. He wondered for a moment if he had failed her.

"He 'will' board MIRROR commander. As will you all. Comrade Voorhies will not be taking Endeavor. I will," pronounced a voice empowered with a self-strength. Stepan Barkov completed his entrance thru the accessway. He needed to slightly bow his head to fit his six foot four frame thru the passage way. His Tokarev pistol gleamed in the lower light of the cabin and appeared larger than it truly was. An older model but deadly by experience.

"Commander Holt I presume? I'd appreciate it if you would place both those weapons on the passenger cushion and step back." Reluctantly, but slowly, Steve placed the weapons on the cushion, but did not move away. He hoped to be able to use them somehow, his thoughts not coming up with a possible solution.

"Let me have my gun," Sid begged and moved to retrieve it.

"Stop! Comrade Voorhies, you will not have any weapons on this station. You may not even stay onboard for long. I have no use for those who betray their comrades." Barkov's distaste for Voorhies' behavior was clearly etched in the Russian's tone.

"Your plan for, how you say, 'asylum' worked perfectly to deliver the Endeavor to me. Now, everyone, move slowly toward the passageway," Stepan demanded. The group did not immediately move, most hoping for some kind of distraction that could be used to grab a weapon that was so close. Finding none, they began to rotate like a dance, the group toward the accessway and Barkov farther inward. Most eyes were on the Tokarev. They continued their little circle dance until the crew was almost outside the accessway and Barkov was standing alone in the middle of the passenger bay. A muffled sound, like steps, echoed into the accessway. Barkov looked out before anyone else could turn around.

A filtered sound spit into the passenger bay. It was unlike any noise Matt ever heard on the Endeavor so he was reasonably certain it did not originate from the shuttle. A dark red spot began spreading on the chest of commander Barkov as he looked down in unbelief, unable to release a sound. As the Russian commander fell, first to his knees, Steve reached out and secured the pistol Barkov was grasping. The Russian then fell backward to the cabin floor. The entire group was stunned, wondering what just happened, as Annushka entered fully into the Endeavor's main bay. She was carrying a pistol/silencer with wisps of smoke releasing from the barrel as the smell of gunpowder attacked their senses.

"I apologize for what my second in command was planning. It was not with my order or approval," she began. "He has not been a settled soul for many years. I think his spirit broke for concern for his family below. I'm not entirely sure, he was a man of few words," she added.

Steve came out of the group funk first and snatched the two weapons on the cushion. Matt pushed Sid past the shoulder of Annushka and disappeared into the accessway. There were muffled voices offered, but nothing that could be understood. Then a louder scuffle and a louder noise. Matt retuned to the cargo bay and explained, "Mr. Voorhies will be temporarily incapacitated for a few hours. A small payment for Miki," he added. Steve was thankful that some measure of justice was meted on the sick bastard, but nothing would truly be justice for the woman he had just met four days ago.

"Janice, please go forward and begin the preflight... 'whatever's' to launch this craft. Matt and I will haul Barkov to his 'homeland' on MIRROR and Matt will join you post haste," he whispered. Janice disappeared in an instant, thankful to be away from the main bay.

Annushka followed behind Steve and Matt as they carried the dead Russian through the inside passageway to the MIRROR receiving corridor. They set him down as carefully if he had been alive, next to an unconscious Sid Voorhies, former employee of SSI. Matt nodded at Annushka as to offer a silent means of thanks. She nodded in return and he headed back to join Janice.

Steve and Annushka stood silent for several moments. Observing each other and downward at the bodies of two men who had little to offer for the good of mankind, they each wondered what serving side by side might have turned out. Annushka re-holstered her weapon that moments ago reduced her command staff by one.

"I can't thank you enough commander. Not only did you save our three lives, but likely the lives of three others onboard PARADISE. I hope you will not suffer any consequences for your actions?" he asked.

"Possibly, but not likely. I'm certain I can weave a compelling story and will recommend Stepan for some kind of service medal. Either way, I can, how you say, 'ride it out,'" she explained.

Steve gazed fondly into the Russian commander's eyes and her countenance softened, to her own surprise.

"You have something to add?" she wondered.

"What about Mr. Voorhies? What's going to happen to him?" Steve inquired. "I guess we could return him to PARADISE, but I'd be thankful if he stayed aboard MIRROR." Annushka gave Steve a contemplated smirk.

"I will make him part of the story surrounding Barkov."

"Are you sure that will work?" Steve pushed for clarification.

"Not one of my monkeys," she responded with a smile. Steve cocked his head and clearly did not fathom what that was supposed to mean. Some Russian idiom?

Annushka smiled knowing the confusion on his face.

"One of my father's old sayings. Not my circus, not my monkeys. Nothing I should worry about outside my responsibility," she explained.

"Hmmm, I like that. I could have used that several times. Mind if I borrow it?" he pleaded.

"My father would be pleased," she offered. Steve thought a moment before he spoke again.

"Commander, I don't know what influence or authority I will have once this mess down below sorts itself out. But I will promise you this. If you ever need a ride back home, I'll stop at nothing to see you and your people get back safely."

"Thank you commander. I believe you will. We have been told the shuttle Nikon would be here by now, but we've received no further word. We 'do' have supplies for several months, as I said, so no immediate worry. Someday I may need to call on your promise, but not soon. I bid you safe journey," she concluded.

Steve gave her a short military salute while wondering if it was even appropriate. He smiled once more and proceeded back to Endeavor. Annushka heard the Endeavor's docking ring cycle close as she pressed the panel switch to close the MIRROR's side of the accessway port.

Finally, she thought. *A man like my father. A man of honor. It is assuring to think there was at least one man to replace the spirit of my father.*

Chapter 22   Tiger's Cave

Endeavor-3 – Pilots Bay   5:31 pm Nov 5

Forty minutes after Steve had given the pilots the 'all clear', the Endeavor was in a glide orbit to return to PARADISE. The commlink had activated and Steve relayed that he was secured in a passenger's seat.

"Home James," was all Matt heard before he cut the remainder of the conversation from his channel. Janice listened to all of it, but there was nothing significant to convey to her senior pilot. It sounded silly but it was likely a way Steve relieved stress. *If anyone needs to do it, it was him*, she thought.

The Endeavor had been on a precise orbiting path to return to PARADISE, as Matt had dropped the shuttle down from the higher orbit of MIRROR station. The commlink came active again, but the additional static indicated it was not from inside the shuttle. The incoming beep repeated again when the channel was not open for external reception. Matt flipped the commlink to open the channel.

"Endeavor3, this is base, please respond," came through both pilot's headsets.

"Base, this is Endeavor, we read you, go ahead," Janice spoke first observing that Matt was still immersed in flight activities as he had not put the Endeavor on autopilot for the return to PARADISE.

"Matt, Janice, this is Ben. We're tracking you on radar. Seems you are returning to PARADISE station? Did all go well?"

"That's a roger," Janice relayed, providing no additional details.

"We have a different destination for you to consider. In fact------I want to recommend it, over," Ben announced.

Matt was concentrating on the engines and flight path, but Ben's unusual request had interrupted his thoughts.

"Pilot, patch Steve back in the main bay into this commlink. He should probably hear this as well," Matt requested, hearing the seriousness in Ben's voice despite the interfering static.

"Go ahead base, we're taking notes," offered Janice, once she had bridged in Steve. More static and then silence as if the link had broken. Then they heard Ben again.

"I just got off the comm with Pavel and gave him an update of what's happening down here. Thought you might want to hear it first-hand as you consider a possible change in flight path. First, the good news concerning the plague. Understand that loss of life is in the millions. The burial detail will last for months and probably years. It's going to be pretty messy down here for quite some time. The disease appears to have mutated and while it is making people wishing they were dead, most are now surviving. It appears that people with any type "O" blood don't die but just got sick as most people are experiencing now. CDC is still scratching their heads on that, but hey, there hopefully will be plenty of time to work out the how's and why's later. Quite a few medical scientists are worried the plague might mutate again and be deadly once more, but until they know more, nobody knows much. The disease did appear to be more active in warmer climates and almost non-existent in artic environments. Once that rumor surfaced, mass migration began north and south depending on which way was closer. While that saved some lives, probably more were lost due to the infection spreading on contact with people movement. Panic prevailed over common sense once again."

Ben paused a moment to give them time to process that chunk of facts. He began again.

"Communications are being restored, both main radio and television, although the primary purpose is to convey plague information and health instructions. No "I Love Lucy" reruns for the foreseeable future."

Janice whispered to Matt, her hand over her mic, "Whose Lucy?" Matt just shook his head and smiled, but offered no answer.

"So, that brings me to a request. How do you feel about a course change and a visit to the SUNSTAR?" he asked.

"Negative without good reason. We've had our fill of station visits already today. Besides, I'm tired and hungry," Matt added.

"And grumpy," Janice chimed in. Matt gave her 'the look', but still briefly smiled, before his serious look returned.

"Matt, here's the deal. We were contacted by the Japanese consortium this morning. It took some time for the details to finally get to me, but they had a request if we had a shuttle in orbit. They launched their shuttle about twelve hours before you did. They had confirmation it had docked on SUNSTAR. There was nominal communication for several hours, but just before station launch, there was no further communication. They fear the worst, but would like some confirmation if possible," Ben finished.

"Based on that information, I might be willing to do some kind of flyby, but I sure don't want to dock there," Matt admitted.

Ben continued, "With their shuttle already docked, that won't be possible anyway. You'd have to position the Endeavor into a stationary parking orbit as close to SUNSTAR as possible and EVA to their main viewing window. Their ground control believes you can see into two main areas of the station. It should be sufficient to learn the station's status. I used the excuse that we likely wouldn't have the fuel to attempt the mission. They immediately countered with an offer. We're authorized to siphon off the LOX on their docked shuttle. It's a pretty worthwhile risk for the reward in my opinion. You can use the extra fuel, but the decision is yours Matt, base over."

"Stand by one." Matt closed his eyes, shook his head and dropped it down. He would have been thankful to return to PARADISE, get a hot meal, some bunk time and begin planning their return to Earth in the next day or so. As several options raced thru his thinking, Matt turned to Janice and asked, "See if Steve will join us here in the pilot's bay."

"You want me to wake him?"

"He's sleeping? How can you tell?"

"Are you kidding me, I can hear him snoring from here!" she replied.

"Ok, ok, leave'm be. Knowing him, he'd offer to paddle to SUNSTAR himself. What do you think?"

"I say go."

"Just like that?"

"Just like that," she repeated his words back with a little more emphasis.

"You understand what this means? One of us has to go EVA, and by one of us, I mean you," he said in as serious a tone he could convey. The rookie pilot gave some serious thought to her next words.

"I'm 'not' saying it's going to be easy, but I 'am' saying I'm not afraid. I EVA to a window, look in, report what I see. The hard part will be the fuel extraction. We may need procedures and guides if their interfaces are not standard, but we can probably use the fuel," she spilled out of breath.

"So you vote go --------no question?" said Matt, searching for some indecision.

"Hey, you know what the Japanese say, 'If you never enter the tiger's cave, you'll never catch its cub.' Nothing ventured, nothing gained," she elaborated.

"So, ------you know Japanese sayings how?"

"I've had many Japanese instructors. After you learn what they want to teach you, then you ask them what you want to know. They appreciate an inquiring mind." Janice knew that there was nothing more to add and sat back into her pilot's seat just now realizing she had been half kneeling and had stretched her shoulder straps to the maximum.

"Endeaver3 to base, over," Matt spoke with little extra emotion.

"Base------receiving you, over," the clear and calm voice of Ben was a balm for the tired soul.

"Ben, do we know if their fuel interfaces are standard? Is there going to be a problem piping their fuel into Endeavor?"

"They say everything is standard, and all the documentation we have says the same. What's your decision?"

"I guess we're sailing for the land of the rising sun. Can you send me the co-ordinates and flight trajectories? I'm so tired I hesitate to trust my calculations," Matt explained.

"Roger that, the co-ordinates and trajectories are uploading now. Keep me informed and especially if you run into some trouble. Base out."

Catching tiger cubs!   Like that sounds easy! Matt thought.

Chapter 23   SUNSTAR Station

<u>**Endeavor-3**</u> – Pilots Bay   6:16 pm Nov 5

"Based on this flight path we will be 'parking' on the starboard side of Endeavor, just off their docked shuttle-------the Wind something?" Janice was asking no one in particular.

Matt thought for a moment trying to recall some buried memory from news reports.

"Remember Sid said they only had one in service, so it has to be the Rising Wind."

Both pilots were silent for the next ten minutes as Matt concentrated on their new flight path and Janice was planning the EVA. Ben had told Matt to stay alert on their approach as several satellites were in near orbit and should be no problem if they were where they were supposed to be. *That was Ben just being Ben*, Matt thought thankfully.

Finally Janice broke the silence for a question.

"What's the length on the EVA tether? I recall it being only about thirty feet," she asked.

"You got me there, but it's no more than thirty feet, why the question?"

"Well, thirty feet would normally be ok, but I've got to go over the Rising Wind to get to the observation window on the SUNSTAR. Thirty feet is not going to cut it. We can't come in from the back side of the station. That's even farther. How do we do this safely?"

Matt sensed it was time to become mentor again. "Ok -----play out the EVA as a vid in your mind. Try to visualize everything, every step, every procedure. How far do you get, what stops you?" Matt offered, still trying to concentrate on the Endeavor's flight screens. Janice closed her eyes and did as Matt had suggested. Somewhere in the depths of her mind she recalled some of the competing shuttles were longer, adding more cargo bay space, but were still the same in width, wing tip to wing tip. She imagined she would be floating over most of the wing area, perhaps with enough leeway; she might be able to see into the shuttle's pilot bay. A good idea if possible, but not the main mission she reminded herself.

"I think I got it! I take two EVA tethers------but I don't link them together. For safety reasons that's why they're only thirty feet long. I glide over to the starboard side of Rising Wind and latch my first tether from the Endeavor to the starboard side of their shuttle, so the tether doesn't float off. Then I latch my suit to the second EVA tether to the same ring. I have another thirty feet which should be more than enough distance to the view window. What do you think?" Janice was brimming with elation.

"Good thinking, but I suggest one major change," Matt offered.

"Latch the second EVA tether, 'before' you detach the first. I'd hate to be the first pilot in SSI history to lose his co-pilot in space. Good job pilot, well thought out. I suggest you head aft and dig out your suit. Have Steve assist you in double checking all the gages on the O-tank. Take the tether from my suit as your second tether." He paused to collect the rest of his thoughts.

"So, a quick look inside the SUNSTAR's view window. Take a small camera and get any pictures, no matter how gruesome. We need to document that we were really there. Lastly, do you remember where the fuel interfaces are located on both shuttles?"

Janice thought a moment and then replied. "Yes sir, bottom of the shuttle, mid-section. The coil length should reach fairly easy."

"All right, mission timeline. Ten minutes from external accessway to station viewing window. Ten minutes back and ten minutes to connect fuel lines. Five minutes to siphon fuel. Ten minutes to disconnect and restore fuel lines. Leave their shuttle tidy as well. Five minutes back inside accessway. That's fifty minutes total. Add ten minutes for something unknown, one hour. You have twice that time in oxygen in your suit, but don't dally! And I 'will' take a ten-five on that pilot."

"Ten-five sir! Permission to give the commander a kiss on the cheek for luck?" she inquired with her best pixie smirk.

"Permission-------granted" Matt almost stuttered, he hadn't processed the request thoroughly.

Once Janice removed her pilot restraints she bent down over Matt and planted a kiss on his lips. It lasted more than a moment. She straightened up and smiled that Janice world class smile with gleaming eyes.

"That was not my cheek," Matt offered in mock protest, clearly pleased.

"I guess I just have to work on my docking maneuvers sir!" Janice beamed and danced out the pilot's bay.

Docking maneuvers indeed, but all Matt could think about for the moment was the sweet taste of peaches on his lips.

Endeavor-3 – Main Bay   6:22 pm Nov 5

Janice hated to wake Steve from his sleep, but followed her orders, recalling that she would need assistance with her suit as Matt had suggested. Despite a sound sleep, Steve was awakened easily. She reviewed the latest bit of news from below, the Japanese mission request and the possibility of adding needed fuel to the Endeavor. Steve listened intently and did not interrupt once, nodding as if each fact was processed and tested for logic. Finally he spoke once he was sure she was finished.

"Matt just agreed to this?" Steve asked as if it was impossible to believe.

"Well----- not whole heartily, but I didn't have to twist his arm either. Ok, I'm going to need some help getting my EVA suit on," she requested as she opened a tall, thin cabinet. She pulled out a white suit. It was labeled 'Wells' with masking tape on the shoulder.

Janice pulled off her shoes, sat down on one of the couches, pushed her feet into the bottom legs of the suit and proceeded to pull the suit up to her mid-torso.

"While I'm wrestling with this suit, pull an EVA tether out of Matt's suit. It should be in the right lower leg zipper pocket," Janice requested. Steve practically dove into the chamber. There was a quiet sound of rustling.

"Found it. Now what do I do with it?" he inquired, still a bit overwhelmed with what this crew was about to attempt.

"Find a small clip bag and put the tether in it. I'll be clipping the bag to my belt." Janice had finally pulled her suit up to just below her neck. She pointed back to the suit cabinet.

"Find my helmet. It should have 'Wells' on it as well." Steve found it velcroed with several straps to the bottom of the cabinet. It took him a full minute to figure out how to release it with the multiple straps guarding it.

"What, no masking tape on this?" Steve asked as he rolled the helmet in his hands. "Hey, it's a lot heavier than it looks." The rookie pilot just shot him a frown.

"Please lift it and carefully place it over my head if you will. You may be COS of PARADISE, but here you are chief valet!" She wanted it to sound more authoritative, but she couldn't help but snicker.

"Yes, commander. I obey commander," Steve was getting into the role reversal. He placed the helmet over her head and rotated it a half turn. "All secure there. How can I serve you further master?" Steve continued the joke.

"Ok, that's enough Gunga Din. Now open the cabinet next to the suits. There should be oxygen packs with straps. There should be four of them. They should all be full, green lit, but make sure. It laches to the back of my suit and the straps secure it. There are three connections, marked O, C and P on the suit. There are three hoses on the O-Tank with the same codes." Steve secured the oxygen tank to her back as requested and connected the three lines. He verified the oxygen levels were still in the green. Janice's helmet began to glow inside with miniature panels and sensor readings.

"Communications are linked, helmet has power," she confirmed.

"Ok, you are good to go," Steve confirmed.

"Thanks, I'm going to sit down here and catch my breath until Matt gives me the go-ahead. Should be only a few more minutes."

Matt coaxed Endeavor to a parking orbit next to the Rising Wind. He wished he had some way to clamp or dock with something, but that was not to be. He set the proximity alarm to the current distance. It would sound an alert if the

Endeavor moved closer or away from the docked shuttle, but not if it moved parallel.

I'll have to monitor that on my own, he imagined.

"You are go for EVA," he broadcasted throughout the shuttle.

Janice opened the inner docking ring door and stepped into the accessway. She then closed the inner door and when sealed, she opened the outer door. She looked into Steve and gave him thumbs up. She turned and looked straight out over the Japanese shuttle wing. Before she stepped out, she latched the bagged tether to Endeavor, then to herself and stepped out on the Rising Wind's wing.

Rising Wind –   6:37 pm Nov 5

Janice stepped carefully, one foot forward, the back foot followed. She made her way to the port side of the main cabin. She was now going to have to crawl up and over the hull. She found it easier than she expected as handholds countered the zero gravity. Once over the hull, she maneuvered slowly down and set foot on the starboard side wing. She realized she was about out of tether line, just as she had figured. Following Matt's advice, she took her own tether line and connected it to the Rising Wind's tether loop. Then she disconnected her tether to the Endeavor and connected it to the same loop on the Japanese shuttle. She turned to face the SUNSTAR. She had a dozen more steps to the end of the starboard wing and then to follow the handholds to the view window. *So far so good.*

"What's your status pilot?" blasted into her helmet.

"Yikes, that's loud. Hold on, let me adjust the volume down. A moment later she spoke into her helmet mic.

"I'm ready to climb the handholds to the view window on SUNSTAR, ----- status good." Her breathing was labored. She was tired before she put the suit on. She remembered her training drills. Spacewalks were not for the fainthearted. She knew of several rookie pilots that were not cleared for EVAs. Good pilots, not good spacewalkers. *Ok, rookie, time to climb,* echoed in her head.

Janice began climbing the handholds. Step, push, grab, pull, repeat. There were only ten handholds to the bottom edge of the view window. Once her helmet reached the top rung, she stepped up once more, so her helmet faceplate was a good foot above the view window. She peered in. **Little light and no movement.**

"Wells here. No life signs, no activity. Very little light. Hold on, my eyes are just now adjusting to the interior. There is just enough light to view the main room. One body on the floor. Can't really tell if male or female. The far interior door has a bit more light. I can see half a body, the top half is lying outside the room. I've taken several pictures; the flash has revealed no additional life."

"Ok pilot, start back," Matt said, "we've documented what they requested."

"Wait a minute. I thought I just saw something move." Janice placed her helmet against the view window in hopes of seeing something else. As she moved back, a face appeared suddenly and stared back at her, pounding on the view window. The young woman was screaming as if Janice could hear her.

"Commander, I've just located a tiger cub. Now what do I do?" She pleaded into her mic. **Now what do I do?**

The young woman continued to pound on the viewing window.

Chapter 24   Tiger Cub

While Janice was peering thru the view window and gripping the handholds, she was so focused on the face of the girl in the station; she did not realize she was floating horizontally. She wanted to step higher before she sensed her feet were no longer on the lower handholds. *OK, this is a problem. Come on girl, no Super Woman heroics.*

At last she managed to restore her last position, but she still had no way to communicate with the woman in SUNSTAR. Her helmet speaker activated.

"Janice, Steve is coming out with your datapad. You can use either the view screen or the translator function on it. While you're dealing with the girl, Steve will take care of the re-fueling. Stand by. I'll be off the comm for a few minutes, helping Steve with his suit." Matt's voice was reassuring considering the situation. She glanced at the internal timer inside her helmet. It was now fifteen minutes into the EVA. She tried to control her breathing, but knew she was close to failing. Minutes seemed like hours. She felt like she was sweating despite the cooling system contained within the suit.

"Janice, Steve will be exiting the shuttle in a few minutes. Should be near you in ten minutes. Endeavor, over."

"Roger. I'm going to have to climb down the handholds. No way Steve can reach me with one tether." When Janice reached the bottom of the hand holds, she stepped back onto the wing of the Rising Wind and sat down. Twelve minutes later as she looked up, Steve was just coming over the main cabin, the tether line trailing behind him. She was about to remark how skillful he seemed to be maneuvering, when the name on the suit caught her attention. It read 'Rogers' in bright red.

"What------- you couldn't find your own suit?" she asked.

"Time was of the essence, girl, and besides, we accidently unloaded my suit with the containers we removed from the shuttle yesterday. Luckily Matt and I are similar in height, weight and surprisingly good looks." She could just barely glimpse the boyish smile thru his faceplate.

"Here's you datapad. If you don't need anything else, I have to wash some windows and fill the tanks." Discerning no change in her demeanor, Steve continued, "Seriously ------- you ok here? Want to trade jobs?"

"I appreciate the offer. Arm wrestling the fuel lines is more taxing than I'm inclined to tackle just now. I just don't know what to do with this woman onboard SUNSTAR," she explained.

"Well, if it's of any consolation, Matt has Ben and Blade---er-- David, trying to solve the problem as well. You may be on the front line, but there's a team behind you. SSI is not in the habit of letting anyone fail. So go up and find out what the situation is in there. I'll join you as soon as I'm done. Matt felt it wise to try and do both things at the same time. Between you and me, I don't think he likes parallel parking without docking." With that, Steve swung around, climbed up and disappeared over the Rising Wind's main cabin.

Janice once more climbed the handholds on the face of SUNSTAR. When she returned to the view window, the woman had disappeared.

Now what? Janice wondered. Two minutes later the woman returned with a similar device as Janice's datapad. **At least she seems more in control of herself.**

The woman typed in English, 'name = Aoki', and placed it against the window.

"Ok guys, we got a name, Aoki. Not sure if it's first or last. Can someone match it against their employee records?" Janice voiced over the commlink. Moments later, for the first time during the EVA, she heard static interference. Then a familiar voice.

"Running it now. No sense waiting on ground." The voice was PARADISE's computer jock, David.

"Aoki Kimura, age twenty four, biological engineer. Should be able to read, write English. She was scheduled to return on this run of their shuttle. Guess her return ticket was cancelled." David's attempt at humor went nowhere.

Just as Steve was locking the fuel sleeve on the Endeavor, he asked a pointed question thru the bridged commlink.

"David, does her information list her blood type?"

"Yep, O positive," came the reply with no delay.

"So. based on what little we know, she likely got sick and recovered, while everyone else died. Janice, see if you can get some confirmation of that?"

Janice typed, 'BLOOD TYPE?'. This time in larger letters to make it easier to read. Aoki nodded and typed 'O' and displayed her tablet back toward Janice.

Janice typed, 'WERE YOU SICK?' and placed it against the view window. This time Aoki just nodded.

The rookie continued typing, "ANYONE ELSE ALIVE?'. The woman looked down for a moment and shook her head slowly. *Maybe she lost someone she was close to?*

'DO YOU HAVE EVA SUIT?' was quickly entered into Janice's datapad. Again, Aoki nodded, but her face could not mask the fear spreading over it. *Aoki, the only way out of SUNSTAR is by spacewalk,* Janice thought, unsure how that was going to happen.

"David, where is SUNSTAR's AAP?" she requested. She waited patiently, but kept looking at her helmet oxygen time, now at fifty seven minutes. She was tiring by the minute. She began to feel as if her own life force was clicking down. David finally came back with detailed information.

"According to their specs, their AAP is the same as PARADISE. Only difference is SUNSTAR has two more levels, and they number them down, not up. The AAP is located center of the bottom level, number eight."

"Can someone EVA from the bottom level to the Rising Wind's wing?" she asked hopefully.

"Depends on their skill level and tether lengths, but it should be possible," came David's reply. Janice thought for a moment. It seemed like she and David were discussing a moonlit stroll across a sandy shore instead of a dangerous walk where a simple slip could end with loss of life and eternally floating in space.

Janice typed, 'PUT EVA SUIT ON' and once more pressed it against the view window. The woman shook her head, clearly afraid of something. Janice shook her datapad as if she was shouting. It seemed the simplest way to demonstrate the seriousness of the request. The woman backed away slowly and once more disappeared.

Twenty minutes later Aoki appeared back at the view window. She was wearing a yellow EVA suit minus a helmet which she carried in her left hand. Janice had already typed out her next message, so she turned the datapad toward the woman. "OPEN AAP?" The younger woman nodded once and for the third time vanished like a puff of smoke.

"Wait, I didn't mention the tether!" Janice shouted, realizing that no one of Japanese descent was listening, only SSI staff. Everyone who heard her remained silent knowing the situation.

"I should come down to the wing, but if Aoki comes back to the view window, no one will be there! What do I do?" Janice's voice was clearly desperate and she started to hyperventilate.

Steve's calmer voice overrode several other sounds in her helmet. "Stay up there in case she comes back". I've completed the re-fueling and I'm just putting the interface hose back in place. I'll come over to the starboard wing to receive her if she shows up there." Five minutes later Steve came over the Rising Wind's main cabin for the second time. The minutes crawled by as Janice kept switching back and forth, observing Steve on the Rising Wind's wing and then back to the view window. More minutes passed. No Aoki. Steve looked up at Janice and shook his head. *There were a number of reasons that may have prevented Aoki from coming thru the AAP. Maybe she couldn't open the AAP, maybe she couldn't get her oxygen tank on, maybe she was just afraid. Maybe the tether was too short. Maybe, maybe, maybe!*

As she looked back down, Steve was just reaching down under the wing of the shuttle. A hand appeared and then another. Finally Steve pulled the woman up between the station and the shuttle and set her down on the wing. She had no tether! He was about to figure out a way to secure her for a moment when she placed her hands down on the wing and he heard a metallic sound. Magnetic gloves! The Japanese girl knew exactly where to place her hands, as most of the shuttle was composite ceramic. Janice climbed down the handholds and wanted to hug the woman; but was afraid to make her break contact with the wing. Steve undid his tether, looped it thru the girl's suit belt and reattached it to his suit. For the first time the woman offered a controlled smile. They all sat there for a few minutes. Steve finally spoke.

"Guess we caught your tiger cub, huh?"

"Now how could you possibly know about that? You were sleeping!" she insisted.

"The commander of station must know all, see all, hear all-------and besides that, Matt told me when he was helping me get this blasted suit on. He thinks pretty highly of you, professionally and otherwise. Ops, he probably just heard that. Go ahead and blush, I would------if I was a girl!" Finally Steve stood up, offered a hand to both women and managed to raise them to their feet.

"Miss Wells, might I suggest you lead the way, we'll keep miss tiger between us until we're safely aboard Endeavor." The hard part was getting over the Rising Wind's main cabin, but once on the other side, it was smooth sailing to their shuttle. Janice thought she could finally breathe deeply as she heard the accessway cycle and pressurize. One by one they stepped into the main cabin. Matt was there to assist with their helmets and O-tanks. Once that was completed he rushed back into the pilot's bay, leaving all three still standing and exhausted. The internal commlink came active.

"Don't bother to take your suits off. Get in a seat and buckle in. I want to get us away from the station ASAP!" came thru the commlink. Janice moved Aoki to a seat and fastened her in. The rookie pilot plopped into a spare seat and was so exhausted she was barely able to fasten her own belt. They heard and then felt the thruster jets moving the shuttle away from the station. Then a quarter G as two of the four engines fired up taking the shuttle, three staff and one tiger cub to PARADISE station. Ten minutes later Matt opened the comm once again to announce, "ETA to PARADISE fifty five minutes." The announcement fell on three suited spacewalkers, all in an exhausted state of unconsciousness.

Chapter 25   Storytellers

Once Endeavor docked with PARADISE the night before, two very tired, nearly sleepwalking humans; filtered thru the accessway. It was already decided that Janice and Aoki would share the guest room that only last night was shared with Laura. Laura would return to her own cabin. Steve and Matt were offered Sid's quarters, but both men declined and said they were too tired to walk that far, maybe tomorrow. Steve said he would bunk with Matt in the Endeavor, same as last night. Pavel and Laura were disappointed having made a special dinner for their 'heroes', but understood. Breakfast would be at 9:00 am for those able to regain consciousness.

Pavel, David, and Laura were seated at the meal table, cups of coffee and sweet rolls half eaten were before them. Matt came shuffling in, there was no life in his face, no energy in his movement. He might not have been able to sit down without the aid of gravity.

"You look like death chewing on a cracker!" Laura laughed. "I'm so sorry commander, you just reminded me of a saying I heard in college when cramming for a test all night long!"

Matt raised his head a little, and spoke barely above a whisper, "I was hoping for some world-class omelets I've heard about. Unfortunately our chef cannot be awakened at this time. Has anyone see Janice?" Everyone shook their heads.

"Ok, here's my suggestion. I say we meet back here in another couple of hours, --------say noonish."

"Of course Matt, you all were going full throttle for more than twelve hours yesterday," Pavel offered. "Get some more sleep. There is nothing going on that can't wait a few more hours. Here, let me help you back to the shuttle."

As Pavel assisted Matt to a standing position. He glanced back at Laura and said," Don't wake anyone, but please check in on Janice and the young woman for me?"

"Will do Matt," Laura said and rose to complete her promise.

PARADISE station – Meal Bay   12:20 pm Nov 6

Sandwiches were placed out on the table along with plates, napkins, and cups. Laura had decided this meal would be a 'picnic' motif. She made tea, lemonade and coffee. She wasn't sure how many more meals would happen on PARADISE so she was determined to make the remaining few memorable. Both Pavel and David had come in early and agreed with her theme, offering to assist. She noticed the difference between the two men immediately. David couldn't do enough to help Pavel. Plus David hardly stopped talking; he continually asked Pavel about various operations of the station and was offering ways the computer systems could be enhanced to make certain operations more streamlined. *What a difference two days make,* she thought, still arranging and rearranging the table, aiming for perfection and settling for neatness.

Janice and Aoki arrived first. Both men rose, but Pavel immediately went to the young girl and offered his hand.

"Welcome, although I'm not sure you can understand me." Aoki nodded and bowed slightly, the usual custom. Janice offered Aoki a seat and sat down beside her. Pavel returned to his seat after refilling his coffee cup.

"From what I can gather, Aoki can read and write English pretty well. She has a speech impediment that prevents her from vocalizing many sounds, Japanese or otherwise. Apparently she is pretty intelligent to still land a space platform research job," Janice boasted about her new friend.

That raised a thought in David's mind.

"Now I understand-------when I was reading her company profile, the language field had Japanese, English and question marks! I thought it was a typo. Her IQ was listed at one hundred fort-five," David explained, clearly impressed.

"And 'who' has an IQ higher than mine?" came blasting thru the corridor before a human shape appeared. Then two tired men, walking slowly but deliberately, emerged into the meal bay. Both sets of eyes focused for an open seat and moved in that direction.

Janice was more than ready for verbal jousting.

"And what is your listed IQ sir?" she asked, looking Steve directly in the eye.

"Wellllll------let's see, it was one hundred thirty before I left Earth. I'm guessing I lost at least four points on the available food around here. Can someone beat that?" He questioned as he sat down with some measure of exaggerated gusto.

Everyone but Matt and Steve pointed their hands at Aoki, who was startled for a second, but seeing the grins on their faces and understanding the gist of the questions, just returned a bemused smile. Steve raised his hands in surrender.

"Ok, are we meeting and then eating or eating then meeting?" Steve asked with a smirk.

"We are eating first and then you can do whatever your little heart desires commander," Laura practically ordered.

"We've made ham and cheese, tuna fish, and chicken for cold sandwiches. The grill is ready; we can make Philly cheese steak, or grilled chicken for hot sandwiches. It's all out on the table. Enjoy."

The discussions started lightly, but Pavel, Laura and David wanted to hear the details on MIRROR and Sid. Steve provided most of the story, filled in bits and pieces with personal observations from Matt and Janice. Pavel was mildly shocked when he learned Annushka had shot Barkov.

"I always admired her. She was constrained to follow regulations imposed on her all her life, but she held her own council of right and wrong," Pavel murmured almost to himself.

"So Sid had smuggled a gun up here?" David couldn't believe it.

"Either he did, or Ripley, or a part at a time. It could have been hidden in the food or medical containers as well," Steve surmised out loud.

"We unloaded together, but Sid always handled the medical container and I was assigned the food. We each had to do an inventory for our area. He would have had free access every time," Laura added.

"That brings us to the SUNSTAR. I heard most of you were bridged in on the audio. Thanks David for your quick response on Aoki." Janice piped up. David just nodded, pleased he could offer assistance.

"I contacted Ben this morning and was able to let Aoki talk to her ground control. Mostly she typed out responses to their questions. Geese, can she type! Since it was all in Japanese I couldn't follow any of it. Ben recorded the data and it was translated for security, since she was on our station. Combined, I think we all figured it out. Someone on the Rising Wind was infected and quickly infected their station. Everyone died in less than a day. Aoki came down sick, but recovered on her own, since she had the O type blood. Something knocked out their communications, probably something as simple as a fuse, but all communication, audio, data, telemetry, et cetra, was all disabled. Probably take David five minutes to get it back up and running, but Aoki had no idea and their comm station office was locked to boot. So, she just waited there, even afraid to eat anything, she had no idea the infection came from their shuttle. She was losing hope until an SSI helmet looked into the view window. The rest you know, except one thing! Aoki's nickname. It's Tiger! Her older brother gave it to her when she was six. Apparently when she couldn't speak clearly it came out as a tiger hiss!" she exclaimed.

"How's that for a coincidence?" Two perplexed faces were staring at her. Pavel and Laura had no idea where this was coming from. Janice was disappointed her revelation had created no reaction. Matt rose from his chair and stood behind Janice, his hands resting on her shoulders.

"OK, tiger catcher. Remember when you first used the term it was just between us. I told Steve about it and apparently no one heard the term at the time of your discovery. But I know that if you had not insisted we visit SUNSTAR, I would have passed on it. She owes her life to your courage." Matt could not have offered any more encouraging words than what he had spoken. He gave her a brief kiss on the cheek and returned to his seat. Aoki, understanding most of the conversation, leaned over and gave Janice another soft kiss of appreciation.

"Hey can anyone get in on this?" David asked hopefully. Seeing the look on Matt's face, he replied, "In a brotherly manner of course."

"I've come to like you David, I'd hate to leave you on PARADISE all by yourself," Matt said in a serious tone, but could not hold back a grin after a few moments.

"Friends, friends-------we've been thru a tough couple of days, time to focus our plans on returning to Earth." Pavel faced Matt directly and continued, "Commander, has base offered any suggestions as to what we can do?"

"Yes. Steve and I spoke with Ben just before coming to lunch. He wants us to stay aboard PARADISE for a couple more days. Things are settling down, but SSI is moving the Texas base to an airfield north of Toronto. Ben said it's been a backup site for the past year. Once he has operations up and running, he believes we should launch and head for the new base. The Canadians have lost less than ten percent of their population, they were holding their boarders closed until the infection mutated and was no longer as deadly. The upper states were pouring across the border at the peak of the contagion, but now it's slowed to a trickle. Ben says they'll go back to the Texas base in about six months to a year depending on several factors. SSI may or may not still be a viable pharmaceutical company, but their shuttle technology can support a number of opportunities. He'll fill in more details later tonight. Everyone's welcome to listen in at twenty hundred hours. Pavel has already set up the meeting in his command center. That's all I got." Matt sat down as Steve rose and faced the group.

"I just wanted to add that I appreciate everything you've done to get us thru this. As Matt said, what SSI is going to look like in the next few months is open to speculation. If I have any say, I'd be looking for people I can trust, and I'm looking at most for them right now." There were brief smiles and nods and most still were processing what the future might hold for them.

"Oh------ and David, I almost forgot. Ben says he wants to talk to you as soon as possible. Seems like SSI might just need a few good computer jocks. He used a different word, but I cleaned it up for the ladies."

"I'll speak to him within the hour, thanks," David mumbled still a little dazed as he trudged out of the meal bay headed to the computer lab.

"Janice, I'll need your assistance on the Endeavor for a bit. We need to reconfigure the main bay for five passengers rather than the two we came up with. Ben has some ideas we need to see if they will work," Matt requested as he started for the accessway.

"You two 'pilots' go on. We four will clean up and prepare the meal of meals for tonight!" Steve boldly stated. Matt looked at Janice and asked," Do you think they can handle it?"

Janice replied, "Yes, I think Laura and Aoki can handle two commanders."

Pavel and Steve looked at each other remarked together, "pilots!" As the two shuttle pilots disappeared, Steve turned to Pavel with a Texas-sized grin.

"Oh Pavel, by the way, do you think your good buddy, Jack Daniels, can stop by for a visit?" Steve asked.

"Yes, there's a very good chance of that," Pavel replied. "A very good chance."

Chapter 26   Shutdown Plans

The six members of SSI, plus their newly acquired visitor had just completed their dinner. The conversations had been little more than small talk, and just below their anxiety was worry for their safety. While Aoki did not participate in the conversations, her apprehension was fueled by the veiled and distant looks she observed in everyone. Something was bothering everyone. The dishes and plates had been moved off to the cleaning sinks, coffee cups and small dessert brownies were all that was still left on the tables. The crews expected an update on their status and Matt and Steve were prepared to provide it and the tasks for the next few days of activities. Matt and Steve slowly stood up and moved to the head of the table, while the rest of the crew remained sitting.

"Ok, friends, here's the latest, direct from our favorite ops manger. Matt do you want to begin from the shuttle viewpoint and I'll finish up?" Steve asked.

"Sure. Well------ Ben and a large group of the remaining staff are en route to a new SSI facility northwest of Toronto. A small town called Sudbury, It's a recently shutdown mid-sized airport. Ben thinks we can use it to land there without too much new construction. The communication links and towers are supposedly still in operation. This will likely be the new North American SSI base for the next year, before returning back to Texas sometime in the future. Ben is planning on our return in a couple of days, once he gets the new location up and running. Laura is assured we have enough supplies for two more weeks, so no issues there. Janice and I have re-configured Endeavor's passenger bay for four passengers. However, someone will have to be strapped back in the cargo bay for the descent in order to get everyone down. We have all the fuel we need thanks to our stop at SUNSTAR. In fact, we may have too much fuel by weight. That's about it from the shuttle side," Matt added.

"In case anyone is wondering, our cargo rider will be Commander Holt, since he has experience riding cargo straps!" Janice offered with her patented pixie smile. A few people smiled as well, but most were not going to be so easily distracted from their concerns.

"Yes, well that was unintended to be sure," Steve remarked.

"Thank you Endeavor. So, that brings us to our tasks for the next couple of days. Laura, please complete any critical experiments or work that can be accomplished in the next two days. Then begin the process of shutting down the labs. If you don't have complete procedures, make them up and document what you have done. It will be critical to know the status of PARADISE as we leave it. Ben is hinting we most likely will not be returning for more than a year." Steve paused a moment to sort thru his thoughts and glanced down at his datapad before beginning again.

"Pavel and David, you two need to prepare PARADISE for shutdown. I've not seen or heard anyone speak in those terms, but again, if there are no procedures, document what you can. While Ben is not going to be much help in this area for the next few days, he assures me he still has competent staff in Texas that can assist you. Don't hesitate to call on them for ideas. I don't need to remind you that PARADISE is a valuable asset to SSI that we will need for the future. Let's make sure it stays in working order. That's pretty much it; I'd like to have short status meetings at dinner to be sure we are on track. If you need me, I'll most likely be with Pavel in the command center, or with David in the computer area. I'm just another set of hands if you need 'em. If there are no questions, this meeting is adjourned."

Several staff started to file out as Steve noticed David and Laura leaving together practically shoulder to shoulder. *Hmmmmm romance in space. It still amazes me how conflict, then cooperation, causes people to see others differently.*

Pavel and Steve were sitting around the command center conference table, each reviewing documents and procedures that had been found, modified, re-written and tested. Steve looked up from his stack and addressed Pavel.

"Pavel, these reports have exceeded my expectations. If I had any concerns about how we were leaving PARADISE, they are gone now. This is simply a great job all around."

"Thanks Steve. I agree, they are doing a thorough job." Both men were mired in thoughts and notations when the commlink buzzed.

"Pavel, is Steve with you? This is David; we may have a serious problem." Steve's head snapped up immediately.

"David, Steve here, what's up?"

"I could try and explain it, but I think you are going to want to see it for yourself."

"Ok, I'm on my way, where are you?" Steve questioned as he rose from the desk.

"In our favorite, full of secrets, lab number 3. I'd hurry; we may not have very much time."

PARADISE station – Lab-3   3:34 pm Nov 7

Three minutes later sporting a flushed face, Steve cautiously strolled into the lab where he saw David, on his knees near an open air vent.

"Is praying going to be a part of the solution to this problem?" Steve joked, but was sorry the minute he said it once he saw the serious look on David's face. Something he hadn't expected to see so soon.

"It might help," David replied and slid aside, still remaining on his knees and motioned for Steve to take a closer look into the vent. The cover was already removed and set aside the lab desk. Steve observed what looked like a small power supply, a metal box about the size of a piece of carry-on luggage and a dozen, multicolored wires growing out in no apparent pattern.

"Tell me that's not what it looks like?" Steve's voice pleaded, knowing the answer that was forthcoming was not going to be assuring.

"Well, I can't tell you anything for sure. I've only had a couple of training sessions involving explosives, but this device looks exactly like some of the training videos I've had. I'm certainly not qualified to disarm it." David said almost apologizing.

"Correct me if I'm wrong but does that seem like a countdown timer?" Steve asked as he pointed to a small LED panel that appeared to be decrementing.

"That would be my guess. It's gone down about six or seven counts since I found it. If those are minutes, then we have fifty nine minutes left I'm afraid," David said not believing the very words he spoke.

"Wait a minute---------how did you find this and what triggered it now?" The commander was struggling, trying to deal with too many random appearing facts.

"And who sets a bomb for what, -------sixty six minutes? It makes no sense!"

David typed a few keys on his datapad and became frustrated when the response was not immediate. The counter was moving, but everything else played out like slow motion video including his thinking. Finally, the screen displayed the information he requested. David just nodded, as if confirming his suspensions.

"As to the who------ how about someone whose employee number is sixty six."

"If I had to guess about that, I'd say, Sid Voorhies."

"Bingo," David said as he held the datapad for Steve to review.

"Alright, we have the who and the what. I'm still confused about how this was activated? Could it have been triggered remotely?" Steve wondered aloud.

"Possible-----but unlikely. Actually, I think I set it off. Accidently of course." David added quickly.

"Ok, I'm listening." Steve braced himself for an explanation.

"Laura and I've been following the procedures for shutting down the labs. She's doing labs one and two. I'm doing labs three and four and then we were to meet and do five and six together. After we check all the gas cylinders, hoses, valves and tanks, the last task is to shut down power to the lab itself, there on the wall panel." David pointed behind the door, as the door partially blocked the panel when fully opened.

"Each lab has its own power feed so it can be shut down without disrupting any other lab. As soon as I pulled the power, I heard a noise coming from the vent. I opened the vent, saw this and called you. My guess is that Sid or whoever, rigged this device to monitor the power in the lab. If the lab's power was cut off, the device triggered. The device has its own power supply for detonation. They probably thought the explosion would cover any tracks they might have left. Plus the explosion would most likely be blamed on faulty shutdown procedures. It's clever any way you look at it. As far as disabling it, there are four red, black and green wires. Most of them are probably false wires for disarming, but any of them could be a trigger to set it off if cut. We just don't know."

"What about moving it, throwing it out the AAP, is that possible?" Steve asked hopefully.

"I moved it several inches when I first found it, but once I realized what it was I stopped immediately. You might be able to move it out of the vent, but if it has any kind of rudimentary motion detection, that could set it off as well. No way will we make it to the AAP down below using the corridor ladder system," David finally added.

"Ok, if you say you can't disable it then we need to be off this station in ------- fifty four minutes," Steve said shaking his head as he gazed at the LED panel. *Is that enough time,* he wondered?

PARADISE station – Meal Bay   3:44 pm Nov 7

The population of PARADISE, minus the shuttle pilots had met in the meal bay in just less than three minutes once Pavel had issued a station wide alarm and request. Worried faces were beginning to be a recurring theme on PARADISE. No one even sat down, perceiving the news to be serious as they looked to Commander Holt for details.

"Ok, I'm afraid there's no easy way to put this. During the shutdown of Lab-3 David found a bomb that is set to detonate in about fifty minutes. I've already alerted the Endeavor crew and they are preparing the shuttle for immediate launch. Round up any documentation, procedures, logs, experiments, et cetra, that you can carry by hand. I'm not going to second guess anyone about personal items, but don't take too long and don't take too much. You have one trip to the shuttle and no more. We need to be onboard Endeavor in fifteen minutes. No time for questions. Now shoo!" The crew scattered like jackrabbits.

I'm supposed to be the COS of PARADISE and several days later it's blown up? That will look just wonderful on my resume. Tell me sir, what was the greatest event during your station command? Well-----my station was in a couple of thousand pieces right before it burned completely up! Steve thought as he headed toward Endeavor shaking his head. *Great resume!*

Chapter 27   Exit Stage Down

Endeavor-3 – Docking ring   3:50 pm Nov 7

As Steve approached the docking ring to Endeavor he met Janice coming out.

"Any problems?" Steve asked hesitantly.

"Nope, no problem. Matt is completing the last set of launch procedures and sent me out to assist anyone with storing what they may have brought. Records, reports, small items go in the container in the main bay, anything larger back in the cargo bay. Then get everyone strapped in, cycle the accessway and report back. Matt says we have ample time, but don't waste any time," she replied.

"Waiting here is killing me. I didn't unload anything of my personal stuff from Endeavor, so I had nothing to bring back aboard. Speaking of that, based on weight, do we need to unload anything of mine?"

"Not if you were under your allowed cargo weight. My question is how are you going to ride this down back in the cargo bay? This is reentry, not a glide across from station to station. Matt said to remind you of that," Janice added.

"Hmmm. I wasn't thinking that through was I? Well, there really isn't an alternative. I want my people safe and secure. I'll take my chances with the cargo bay. If you get the Endeavor down in one piece I should be ok." They both stood there for another few minutes not saying anything, lost in their own private thoughts.

The first group that came thru the accessway was Laura and Aoki pulling a large case on wheels. Before Janice or Steve could object, Laura shouted out first.

"Don't worry! I don't want to take this cart. We just threw everything we needed into it to make it easier to bring to the shuttle. It's less than half full!" Once they stopped at the docking ring and caught their breath, Steve and Janice had already opened the case and began pulling out the contents. Everyone grabbed a handful and proceeded into the bay to unload into the prepared container.

"Ok-------Laura you're in the right front seat, and I'll get Aoki strapped into the other front seat. Just as Janice had finished securing Aoki and checked Laura's straps, Pavel rushed in, his face pale, pasty. Perspiration was streaking across his forehead before he wiped it with his sleeve. He was carrying a small suitcase with personal effects in one hand and a briefcase in the other.

"Permission to come aboard?" he asked quietly. Before Steve could answer Janice spoke up.

"There may be a twenty four hour delay period," she said, a serious look on her face as she peered directly into the Russian's sad eyes.

"I guess I had that coming," the words barely out as the aged Russian looked down. There was no movement for several seconds. Everyone was holding their breaths racing to imagine what was coming next.

Janice slowly went to the elderly man, and hugged him.

"No you didn't. You did what you thought was right. You could have explained it better though," she explained with a smile. "Welcome aboard commander. You have the second starboard seat behind Laura. David will be in the one next to you behind Aoki. Now we're just waiting on David."

Steve was outside the Endeavor docking ring pacing furiously back and forth when Janice emerged. The look of frustration was layered on his face.

"Everyone but David is here----------but you already knew that", Janice offered without trying to express the obvious which she did already.

"Where is he? He's had more than enough time to round up anything he needed to return to base-------this is starting to make me angry!"

"I think you flew past angry two minutes ago. If it helps I'll pace too!"

With that response Steve stopped in his tracks, looked at the rookie pilot and just shook his head. "You have a way with words, I'll give you that. Ok, no sense us both wasting time here waiting. Go back to Matt and assist him anyway you can. Tell him we're just waiting on David. I'll get him secured, close the docking ring, and cycle the accessway myself. Once everything is good in the main bay, I'll head to the cargo bay and commlink when I'm settled and secured." Janice listened to the commander's checklist, mentally verified all the procedures and gave him thumbs up.

"Roger that commander, and don't bite David's head off when he shows up. Bet he has a good reason for taking as long as he has." Janice winked at the commander and like a wisp of smoke vanished into the shuttle, while the simmering volcano of a commander returned to his determined pacing. Four more impatient minutes passed and finally Steve thought he heard footsteps in the far corridor. Seconds later, David appeared, he was struggling to carry an electronic device of some kind and a brief case similar to Pavel's. He was wallowing back and forth like a six foot penguin. Steve waited until David was beside before he blew up.

"Where in the hell have you been? We should have left almost five minutes ago! I thought I made myself pretty clear to get back here pronto."

"You did. I was ready in about one minute with the gear I was bringing back. Then I got an idea on hopefully how to save PARADISE." That revelation stopped Steve in his tracks. The idea that PARADISE might survive somehow filled him with a hope he had buried minutes ago.

"So give----what is this idea?"

"Really commander, it's already done if it works. Don't you think we should be launching as soon as possible? I'll fill you in on the ground." Having said that David ducked into the docking ring and unloaded his offerings to the Earth container. He took the only available seat and while he was struggling with the safety straps, Steve closed the docking ring on the shuttle side and secured it. He pressed the accessway panel switch and the familiar hiss and orange light confirmed it had cycled and sealed properly. He moved to assist David and completed locking his straps and positioning them correctly crossed over his shoulders.

"Everyone stay seated, listen for any instructions from Matt on the commlink and I'll see you on the ground." Steve hoped this last set of words would be received in the calming manner he offered them. He double checked everyone's straps and headed aft into the cargo bay.

"Matt------all passengers and cargo secured. You are----
go to detach from PARADISE. I'm guessing we have ------less
than thirty minutes until -----detonation. I'd start -----pedaling."
Steve's harried voice came thru the commlink in chunks, as he
was fast running out of breath. Each set of passengers looked
at their respective row partner and tried to give some
indication of bravery. But no one saw what they wanted in
each other's eyes. Matt toggled his commlink thru the shuttle.

"We will detach and thrust away from PARADISE in
thirty seconds. Be sure you are secure in your seat. The
decent should be similar to any prior flights you have
experienced before, but we are landing at a new base in
Canada and we have full tanks, both are new parameters.
Hopefully the runway is long enough. Stand by to detach."

"Pre-flight checks complete, ready for detach," Janice
replied by rote. Matt had to remind himself that while he had
experienced almost fifty Earth target flights; this would be
Janice's first.   Still, she had displayed how professional she
was in these last trying days. Matt expected no less today.

"Release docking clamps," Matt requested.

"Docking clamps released," resounded in his headset.
He only had a moment to offer up a smile to the rookie. She
seemed to know it was there and in smiling back, she showed
her own appreciation for his leadership.

"Starboard thrusters -----standard one quarter."

"Clearing PARADISE station----station clear," the rookie
imparted as the skilled pilot she had become. By procedure
she viewed the starboard camera and proximity screens to
provide shuttle positioning to the senior pilot.

"Aft thrusters one quarter until clear of orbiting station
by one kilometer."

"Point three....point five....point nine.....one kilometer
and more clear," rang thru Matt's headset. He fired the main
engines and Endeavor began the first of three spiraling
revolutions before it would level off over the Baja coast.

"Endeavor 3 to base." Matt waited ten seconds before
repeating.

"Endeavor 3 to base, come in."

"Base here. This is Johnson, go ahead ,over."

"Ben, hadn't heard your voice since you were in Texas. How's the weather there in ------what's this placed called again?"

"Its old name is Sudbury, but we call it SSI North, and damn glad to be here. It's cold Matt, but at least it's dry. We didn't add any more concrete, but if you run out of runway the area is clear for several miles and flat. We read you moving out of PARADISE orbit, confirm, over."

"Detached approximately five minutes ago. After we level out over the Baja, it seems like the same trajectory path to SSI Texas," Matt inquired.

"Correct, only you stay at the same level until you reach Texas. Then turn north forty nine degrees to the Canadian border. Your path will take you over Lake Huron. Once there you'll need to reduce engines and apply flaps to reduce speed. You'll then fly over the Georgian Bay. You have about fifty miles to base. The tracking signal is the same as Texas, we brought all that gear with us. Sorry I didn't have time to program a computer flight plan. We're still walking on top of cables and sitting on boxes, but we are up and running. Wind is out of the north east at fifteen. We'll start breathing again once you are down. Ben out."

On the second downward rotation, Janice thought she saw a bright light just as the shuttle continued its homeward trajectory. She inched up in her seat to look over her shoulder but the Earth's bright face was now in the way.

"I think I saw the explosion of PARADISE------I can't be sure. Just saw a flash, but it had to be it. Co-ordinates are on target. I feel bad for Steve," she added. Matt broke thru her comments.

"If it's true, I feel bad for all of us. But push that out of your thoughts for now, we're coming up on last rotation and brake over Baja and final glide path. Keep feeding me altitude and speed in that order. I have eyes on telemetry tracking and flight path. Actually gliding the shuttle is somewhat harder but actually more fun. Having the extra fuel makes it more sluggish but probably smoother." The shuttle braked over Baja and blistered over the northern territory of Mexico until it reached the western portion of Texas. Matt began a small northern arc heading directly over Dallas as they proceeded to the Great Lakes. The Endeavor passed just east of Chicago and flew over the U.P or the Upper Peninsula as the residents of Michigan lovingly refer to it. Endeavor entered the Canadian airspace once it passed the midpoint of Lake Huron. Matt began the breaking procedure and the shuttle began to buckle and bounce a few seconds before settling down. They quickly crossed Lake Huron and were over the Georgian Bay. Matt continued the braking procedure and heard the tracking signal begin to sound indicating they were on track.

"Full flaps-----thruster engines off, -------on glide." The slight bump and buckle continued for another minute.

"There's the runway. Alignment looks good, nose a bit high, altitude one hundred feet, speed 210," Janice reported.

"Correcting------nose lowered. Deploy drag chute when wheels down------now."

"Landing gear down and locked."

"Chute   deployed-------speed   150-------130-----120", Janice's voice was getting desperate. They were slowing, but quickly running out of runway.

"I see it--------speed?" Matt yelled

"100--------90". Matt toggled the commlink.

"Team, brace for impact, we're running out of runway."

Matt focused on keeping the shuttle as centered on the runway as possible. He could see nothing in front of him and he wanted to keep it that way.

"Speed 40," Janice stated just as the shuttle escaped the end of the plowed runway. *At least there was no barrier or fence* Matt thought. He expected a rough and bumpy ride, but instead the shuttle just literally plowed thru a series of snowbanks just three feet high. They rolled another two hundred feet, but the journey was as smooth as glass. The blue drag chute flopped down as if shot as soon as the shuttle stopped rolling.

"Endeavor to base, we have landed or something."

"Base here. It appeared more to me like you landed, bounced, skidded and snow plowed. I'm not sure we're paying for that one. Everyone ok?"

"What in the heck is out here after the runway? It was smooth," Matt asked as he began to remove his seat harness.

"You mean the town's ice skating rink? It was built before the runway, but shutdown when the airport opened. Then it reopened when the airport was shutdown two years ago. It's three inches of solid ice over concrete, almost the width of the runway and almost three hundred feet. They said they could hold three junior hockey matches at the same time. Security has been keeping everyone off it since we bought the facility. We were going to plow it, but thought if you needed it, the snow would help slow you down. Worked didn't it?" Ben could hardly hold in his laugh.

"You could have told me!"

"Naa, it was better you thought you had the runway you saw. Hey, who's the safety OPS guy here?"

"SSI will be short one safety guy if I ever get my hands around his neck. Endeavor over and out!" With that, Matt cut all engine and instrumentation power.

Matt turned to his co-pilot and issued his last command for the day, "Let's get our passengers out and call this a day!"

"Ten-five there commander!" As Janice whisked back to the main cabin, Matt slumped back in his seat a moment and gave silent thanks for all his flight training and a certain friend's safety planning.

Chapter 28   Debriefing

As members of the Endeavor's last flight filed in, James Donaldson and Ben Johnson greeted them one by one with a handshake and warm appreciation for their last few days of service. Most stopped at the breakfast bar, and loaded up a plate and something to drink, either coffee, tea, juice or both.

Matt had arrived early before everyone and was standing at the large window on the second floor looking out at the Endeavor. It was still out two hundred feet off the runway. It had not been moved since yesterday, and a small amount of snow dusted the wings just enough to obscure the SSI logo. Ben came up behind him, placed an arm on his shoulder and spoke quietly.

"She's one heck of a machine. Glad you got her down so well. We've never really tested the reentry aerodynamics with a full fuel tank. We're scheduled to move her late today or early tomorrow and get her inside the main hanger."

Matt kept his focus on the shuttle, but offered, "Yes, she performed beautifully. I'll be adding that in my report that she flew smoother with the extra fuel. Maybe we can add some weight without fuel. I know that wastes fuel, but might be safer. It just handled so well. It's a pilot's thing."

"Then be sure to add it. We'll look into what we can do. But for now, let's get this debriefing over and start rebuilding the new direction of SSI."

Ben waited until all were seated before he offered to introduce Director Donaldson to the group, as most had not met him before.

"Well ----we need to get started. We're missing Steve Holt and our Japanese friend, Aoki Kimura. Perhaps they will join us soon. James, this is the crew of Endeavor 3." Both Matt and Janice raised their hands as Ben directed his gaze toward them. "The crew of PARADISE station." Pavel and Laura meekly raised their hands momentarily. David was unsure what to do with his hand, so it remained holding his coffee.

"For those who don't know him. I'd like to introduce Director James Donaldson. Steve, Pavel and I report directly to him as do a number of other departments. Director, you have the floor." Ben sat down and the director stood up, took a sip of coffee and glanced at everyone before he began. There was some slight tension as most did not know what to expect for this meeting.

"I hope everyone got a good night's sleep. I asked Ben to schedule this short meeting. I wanted to go over a few notes before you start your respective reports. Basically to ensure what things need to be in there and what issues, ----- may be best left out. Let me assure you of one thing, whatever you submit will not be edited. Your report will be your report, unchanged. This meeting is to clarify a few things and for you decide what you may or may not include in your reports." With that, Donaldson sat back down.

He continued, "Ok, if there are no questions from you all, I'd like to ask a few questions and we'll see where this goes. Ben, can you give us a status on PARADISE station?"

"Well, best I can with some limited information. We can track that PARADISE is still in a stable orbit. We have limited technical status as PARADISE was put into a shutdown mode to conserve battery life since we weren't sure when we would be going back. We're getting status on minor readings which indicate the comm transmitters are fine and power is stable. I just got a report this morning that optical observations show the station slightly tilted and one lab appears to be gone." David raised his hand. Ben recognized him with a nod for him to provide his input.

"I think I can offer some information on what you are seeing," he said.

"Well I certainly hope so," came from the main door as Steve entered and sat down next to Pavel. I've been waiting a day to hear this." All eyes shifted from Steve back to the computer expert. He swallowed quickly and tried not to show his nervousness, but Steve gave him an encouraging smile.

"Most of you know we discovered a bomb in Lab-3 inside a vent. We suspected Sid based on a number of things---- no need to go into those now. We didn't feel we could disarm it, so Steve called for the immediate evacuation of the station. Once I rounded up what I was going to bring back I got a wild idea. There was no time to discuss it, and it was a bit fool hardy on my part, I admit now. I could have been blown up and risked the shuttle's safety as well. I was pretty sure we couldn't move the bomb to the AAP, but I was confident if the device detonated where it was, the main gas lines and fuel lines would have been toast. The station would likely have been destroyed. I took the risk to move the device from the vent and placed it on a cart. I moved the cart to the extreme part of the lab, near the far window. I placed several steel cabinets behind it to shield the station. I hoped when the bomb went off, it would deflect mostly outward. Certainly destroy Lab-3, but maybe save the station. Anyway, that's what I did. I hope it paid off," he added lastly. It took a moment for most to process the details David alluded to. They were trying to visualize his actions.

"I think you very well saved PARADISE. That was as brave and foolish as anything I've heard of in a long time," Ben explained. "Well done son." There were nods of agreement around the table.

"Am I to understand that David doesn't even work for SSI?" Donaldson asked as he looked thru his notes.

"Not at the time of his heroic efforts, but I've made him an offer this morning. I think he can upgrade our computer networks both land and space based," Ben piped up. What do you say son?" David was momentarily caught off guard.

"Give me one more day to make a final decision, but I am sure leaning with SSI. I've given it a lot of thought and I guess I'm tired of playing undercover characters in my security role. I'd rather just be me. I have a ton of ideas to try on PARADISE that I worked out with Pavel our short time there at the end. As long as I don't have to go back into orbit!" David leaned back as if a tremendous weight had been lifted.

"Speaking of Mr. Oberholtz. Pavel, I promise you that will be the last time I ever use your last name," Donaldson apologized.

"First, all the accusations concerning your activities have been cleared. We now know what Mr. Voorhies was doing to frame you. Steve and I discussed a number of issues last night and COS of PARADISE is no longer on his career path. He recommended we ask you to return as COS as soon as we restart our space operations on PARADISE. Sorry I didn't get a chance to ask you in private, but I assume you are comfortable with this group considering what you have gone thru together?"

"Yes, yes----I'd welcome the chance to get PARADISE back into operations. I've learned a lot about working with people thanks to most of these here," Pavel said as he waved his arm from side to side. "I think this gentleman," as he pointed to David, "will be invaluable to create and secure our space networks. I will apply some Russian persuasion to bring him aboard!" Quick smiles abounded again, but no one was sure what was coming next.

"Since I appear to be the moderator of this meeting, I guess I want to hear from you next, Steve. What's the latest news from your perspective?" Donaldson inquired.
The whole group unconsciously sat up straighter. For some reason everyone felt his comments would be the most interesting.

"First, I want to second Ben's opinion on what David did to save PARADISE. If he had asked me first, I would not have approved and we would have lost a valuable resource. But, never forget, our people are our most valuable resource. If we forget that once or twice, we've already lost the company." Steve paused a moment to gather his thoughts as to what to share with the group and what to reveal to his management only. He began again.

"I apologize for being late; I had my time zones mixed up. I had scheduled a commlink call to MIRROR station and well, let's just say, we had a few glitches. Anyway I was able to speak with Commander Rusnak for a few minutes. I was following up on a promise I made to her. The good news is their main shuttle is about ready for launch and she expects they will be relieved next week. All is well aboard. She confessed there was no injured person and that it was ruse by Barkov to get Voorhies aboard MIRROR. What Voorhies didn't know, was it was a ruse by Barkov to get Endeavor 3 to their station. The best news of all is that upon returning to the Soviet motherland, Mr. Voorhies will be tried for the murder of Barkov." That revelation had everyone scratching their brains trying to piece what details had already been revealed concerning the Endeavor's docking experience at MIRROR.

"I know, I know. Rusnak is the one who shot Barkov. She had a story already in place, with a medal recommendation for her second in command. But her official story now, once I shared what Sid had done to Miki, was to place that murder on him. It's her word against his-----and ours if we are officially asked. Who are they going to believe? A valued space commander or an industrial spy slash traitor? She promised she will recommend life imprisonment, but it's unknown what the government will decide. That will be out of her hands. I felt it was adequate compensation for what he did to Miki. There was nothing SSI could do to him. We're going to list Miki's death as unknown, and for the most part, that's true. SSI headquarters said they are processing compensation for her family."

"What's become of Aoki, our own little tiger?" Janice inquired with a bit of motherly interest. She had been concerned about the girl ever since they landed and a group of men whisked her off and she hadn't been seen since. Steve was sure Janice was going to ask about their rescued friend, so he had stopped earlier to get details.

"Good question. She is fine, really. The medical staff wanted to examine her first for any signs or conditions of the plague. She was the only survivor aboard SUNSTAR, and they are sure it's related to her blood type. She'll be with us a few days and you'll have plenty of time to see her. The conglomerate from SUNSTAR is arranging passage for her back to Japan as we speak. She may not feel like it, but she'll likely be treated as a hero. The hold-up for her return is international travel limitations. Worldwide there are new procedures going into effect. Type-O will be able to travel without issue, but you know people will try and forge false IDs to get around. It will be five or six weeks before Aoki will be returned to her family. Most likely they will be sending a private boat which I understand is how most travel will be accomplished for the next year or so. I'll take you over to medical this afternoon and you can see her."

"Thanks. I just want to be sure she's safe and not afraid," Janice offered.

"So, Laura, is there anything you want to add to our debriefing?" Donaldson asked, checking off another item in his notes. Laura had hoped she would be allowed to remain silent, but thought this might be the opportunity to map out her next couple of years. In the last twenty-four hours she seemed to find some new direction and spirit.

"I don't have anything to clear up concerning our last few days on PARADISE, but I have been going over Sid's final set of experiments and papers. There are some amazing things he was onto concerning microbiology that nobody else was looking into. I've proposed a new team to focus exclusively on this area and I'm sure it will branch into the plaque research that is going to need a lot of work. Management is just waiting for my final paper to begin evaluating my proposal. If Sid had only stayed the course I believe he would have been SSI's number one research specialist and in the top ten of the industry. I don't know that I can add anything else, but I want to thank you all for the team work these past few days." Laura concluded her words and needed a moment to wipe her eyes just a bit as she sat back down.

"That leaves us with only our pilots to hear from." Donaldson made one last mark in his notes and closed them.

"I defer to my senior commander," Janice quickly stated. She was not prepared nor wanted to share anything personal concerning the last few days for the moment.

"Not sure what the near future holds for me," Matt began. "If we don't return to PARADISE for a year, then we have too many pilots for just zero gravity orbital flights. I've been approached by MIRROR and SUNSTAR to consult on pilot training, procedures, and safety policies. We need to have more common interfaces, commlink controls, et cetera. When there's an emergency on a station, we need better ways to ensure the safety of staff on all of them. I'm working on an idea for a mini-platform that will hold fuel, air and supplies, maintained as a co-operative for anyone in need in space. Of course funding will be an issue, but both groups have said they are interested. I'm thinking of taking a year sabbatical from SSI and see what I can do to get the current stations, and new ones being planned, to work together better. What research they do will continue to be their proprietary business, but space is too big to be out there working independently. That's all I have." Ben stood up with a look of pride on his face.

"Matt, you sound more like me every day. I'll certainly approve that leave of absence. The more each of these companies work together, the safer it will be for all of us. I think that's a fine goal. I wish you the best and you know I will assist you with anything you need from SSI."

"Ok, everyone. I thank you for your time here today. Please stop in HR sometime this morning for paperwork, pictures and new badges. You are dismissed."

David turned to Laura as they rose from the table and said, "Mind if I hang out with you until they find some place for me?"

"Sure. But I warn you, all I have is one table, two chairs, no waste basket, no phone, and a dozen boxes of lab equipment." Laura's face portrayed the slightest look of needfulness.

David smiled. "It sounds like you need someone to unbox and set up your lab. For the time being, I need a job and I work pretty reasonable!"

"You're hired! Follow me." They practically flew out the conference door.

Ben just shook his head with a grin spreading across his face. He looked at Steve and said,

"I offered him a real job and a real salary, and he accepts her offer for nothing!"

"Yeah, well she wasn't offering nothing and you can't offer anything like it. I'm sure in a day or so when all the boxes are unpacked, he'll be looking for a way to stay around here and your job offer will be his ticket," Steve explained as they exited the conference room. Pavel and Donaldson left a few seconds behind them, discussing new ideas for restructuring SSI for the next year. A hospitality clean-up crew removed all the dishes and food items and a few minutes later, only Matt and Janice were left in the conference room. The quiet was almost eerie.

She followed him over to the conference window. Matt and she watched as crews were hitching converted baggage haulers to the Endeavor to bring it out of the field and into a hanger.

"So, your announcement of leaving SSI caught me off guard. Didn't see that coming," she spoke barely above a whisper despite the fact they were alone.

"Neither did I, frankly. It just seemed like a step that needed to be taken and I was the one best suited to take it. What about you? I noticed you didn't share anything during the meeting and that's not like you either."

"I had too many conflicting thoughts, not sure what was important or not. Where will you be going first?" she asked.

"Nothing's been settled, but likely the Russian city of Tyuratam. I'm supposed to meet their officials at the Baikonur Cosmodome in a few months. Who knows how I'll get there, probably by video contact if travel is not restored."

"I've never been to Russia. Wouldn't mind seeing some of that country."

"Oh really? Just up and leave SSI with no prospects, no job?" Janice placed her arms around Matt's neck and looked directly into his eyes.

"I've heard it's been done before. Maybe no job, but I certainly have prospects." With those final words, they embraced each other, and a long lingering kiss commenced.

Outside, the workers were still struggling with pulling Endeavor out of the snow bank. Somehow it was obliviously to the two pilots in the second floor window.

Epilogue

Four days later the shuttle Nikon docked at MIRROR station. It remained less than twenty four hours. The company released no official status of which crew members arrived or returned to Earth.

Soviet media related a small announcement on the death of Stepan Barkov. No details were provided; his family took possession of his body for burial in the family plot near the Baltic Sea.

No announcement was ever provided for the status of Sidney Voorhies, former SSI employee. Presumed lost in space.

SSI provided Miki Yew's family with her possessions left on Paradise and at the Texas facility. Compensation for her death was not disclosed for legal reasons.

Aoki Kimura was reunited with her family seventy three days after returning from space. Despite her reluctance, she was declared a national hero.

Steven Holt formed a non-profit organization called "Ambassadors in Space". The mission statement purported to co-ordinate commerce, safety and cooperation between space-based companies. The first two employees were Matthew Rogers and Janice Wells.

The plague was eventually determined to be man-made, but both the WorldHealth and CDC reported if it had not mutated, nearly seventy percent of the world population might have been lost. Mankind finally saw it's frailness up close. Governments took notice.

The end